OH, BROTHER

Look for these and
other APPLE PAPERBACKS
in your local bookstore!

The Lemonade Trick
by Scott Corbett

The Mystery of the Missing Treasure
by Janet Lorimer

Sixth-Grade Sleepover
by Eve Bunting

The Mall from Outer Space
by Todd Strasser

Short Season
by Scott Eller

No Coins, Please
by Gordon Korman

OH, BROTHER

Johnniece Marshall Wilson

AN
APPLE
PAPERBACK

SCHOLASTIC INC.
New York Toronto London Auckland Sydney

ISBN 0-590-41001-6

31 30 29 28 27 26 25 24 23   4 5 6 7 8 9/0

Printed in the U.S.A.   40

First Scholastic printing, January 1988

This book is dedicated to my father,
John Morley Marshall, Jr.
And to the memory of my mother,
Essie Campbell Marshall.

One

It was a warm, breezy, late spring afternoon. Me and Andrew were trying to get in some hoops before I left to throw papers. My brother, Andrew, shot hoops like a pro. He was winning, of course. I couldn't shoot hoops anywhere near as good as he could. "Ow!" I said, and frowned when he sank another basket.

"That's how the pros do it," he said, grinning.

"You going over to the lot?" I asked.

"I might," he said. "Why?"

"I thought we could finish up this game when I get back from throwing papers."

He didn't say anything. He dribbled the ball on the driveway in front of the garage. He did a lot of fancy dribbles that I could only stand there wishing I knew how to do.

"Since I got a bicycle, it won't take long."

"Come over to the lot when you get back," he said, and tossed the ball into the garage.

I went into the house to get the canvas sack I use to carry my papers. I wasn't in the house very long 'cause the sack was always on a hook in the kitchen utility closet.

When I got back outside to the garage, my bike wasn't there. Andrew had it again. I went 'round to the front stoop and looked across at the vacant lot. The lot was across the street and up the block from my house, but you could see it clear from the front stoop. There were a lot of guys over there playing football, but no Andrew.

I put the sack on the stoop and went upstairs to get some money. Since my bike was gone, I'd need money for the bus.

In my room, I opened the closet door, pushed the clothes to one side. There was a space in the back of the closet wall where the plaster was chipped off and bare brick was showing. Two of the bricks were cemented together, but not to the ones surrounding them. I slipped them out.

The jar was still there. I don't know where I expected it to be. It was just a pint-sized plastic orange juice jar. I took it out.

I slipped out two-fifty, screwed the cap back on the jar, and returned it to its hiding place.

Ten minutes later I was at the bus stop, boarding the bus to deliver my papers.

I settled in for the long ride. Delivering papers on the bus is only hard because there is so much travel time. Good thing the bus was air-conditioned.

Later that evening when I got home, Andrew still hadn't come back. Mama, Daddy, and Bonnie weren't there, either. A note propped against the sugar bowl said they'd gone to the market. There was one paper left in the canvas sack. I pitched it onto a kitchen chair.

Yanking the refrigerator door a little too hard, I grabbed a quart of milk and filled a glass. I took the glass into the living room. I stood in the doorway and looked across the street at the vacant lot. It was Andrew's favorite hangout. It seemed strange for him not to be there.

After I finished the milk, I took the glass into the kitchen and rinsed it. Then I remembered the last paper. An elderly lady, Mrs. Pettaway, always buys a paper from me if I have any left over. I think she just wants an excuse to get me over there to read to her. She must be lonesome living by herself like that.

I cut across our front yard and took the paper to Mrs. Pettaway. She lives in a white aluminum-sided house next door. Her house is set farther back than ours.

I usually read to Mrs. Pettaway since Andrew'd stopped doing it. He stopped reading to her last summer, and I've been doing it ever since. But I was too tired to read to her today.

I didn't go up on her porch. I stood in her yard and tossed the rolled newspaper against her screen door. It made a loud racket and I knew, although she was almost deaf, she'd hear it.

I went up to my room to finish my homework.

Before I got too settled, the storm door opened. It was Mama, Daddy, and Bonnie. I could tell by their footsteps. Bonnie was running and shouting; glad to be home, I guess.

I went downstairs.

"Hi," I said.

"Hello, son," Mama said. "I didn't think you'd be home. I didn't see your bike."

"Andrew borrowed it again."

"I thought he's stopped taking your bike."

"Was that before or after you'd delivered your papers?" Daddy asked, giving me a pat on the head like he did with Bonnie. I thought I was too big to get patted on the head, but I didn't duck down like Andrew would've.

"Before."

"I told that boy to leave your bike alone in the evenings," Mama said, setting a bag of groceries on the table. "Did you fix yourself a snack?"

"Just milk. I got to finish my arithmetic homework. I better go get started." To Bonnie I said, "Come on. Come upstairs with me." I took her hand and led her to the stairs.

4

When I sat to my desk, I couldn't concentrate on homework. I turned 'round to where Bonnie played with a giant coloring book.

"Girl, what did you do all day?"

"Store," she answered. "Crayons, Alex." She sat on one half of the wide coloring book so it'd stay open. "I want crayons."

I wasn't sure I should give her a crayon. Last time, me and Andrew didn't watch her while she colored, and she colored the living room wall. We had a hard time scrubbing that wall.

I gave her two fat crayons. "Just color on paper, hear."

Bonnie laughed and started coloring in her book.

Just as Mama called me and Bonnie down to dinner, I heard Andrew's whistle. It was a fast, happy tune, like birds in the evening before the sun goes down.

I waited in the living room till he came in.

"Don't get mad. I put it in the garage."

"Don't take my bike again, Andrew."

"I brought it back safe and sound."

"I had to ride the bus to deliver my papers. That costs almost three dollars. How much money you think I make throwing papers?"

He walked toward the kitchen. I grabbed him, spun him 'round to face me.

He shook my hand off. I grabbed him again.

He put his left arm around my neck, flung me on the sofa. I fell against the sofa so hard the

5

painting on the wall above it teetered, then fell behind the sofa.

"Boys! Boys!" Mama yelled, coming in from the kitchen. "Let's stop that right now."

We quieted down, but I was still upset. Mama stood in the doorway, looking from me to Andrew and back again, her hands on her hips.

Daddy came out of the kitchen and stood beside Mama. "Andrew, don't bother Alex's bike again. He needs it to throw his papers. Wait until he gets back. Why don't you get a route or something — "

Andrew cut in, "Daddy, I don't wanna. It's too much walking — "

"Too much working, you mean," Daddy said. "Look, there's a time for recreation. In fact, we all need it. But, if you worked after school, it'd round you out. There'd be plenty of time left over for playing football with Mungo and Sammy and the rest of the gang. Do you hear me?"

Andrew nodded.

"Don't nod. You've got a mouth, use it."

"Yes, sir," Andrew said.

"All right. When Alex gets ready to deliver papers tomorrow, where will his bike be?"

"In the garage," Andrew said.

Daddy went and picked up the painting and hung it back on the wall.

I got off the sofa and tucked my shirt back into

my jeans. Andrew went upstairs. Soon, I heard the bedroom door close.

"Andrew," Mama called as she went to the bottom of the stairs, "we're ready to eat."

When we were seated to the table, I looked across at Andrew. He sat silent, eating. Bonnie was in her high chair, mostly pushing food 'round on her plate.

"Listen, Andrew," I said. "You can use my bike long as you want, *after* I deliver papers. Not before."

He looked down at his plate.

"Andrew — " Mama said, then stopped.

"I didn't hurt his rusted old bike." He jumped up so fast his chair slid back and banged the refrigerator door.

"Boy, don't go knocking furniture 'round like that. Sit down and finish your dinner," Daddy said.

Right then, I felt kind of bad for Andrew. He kept getting hollered at, all because of me. But it was my bike and I did need it.

Andrew sat down again.

We finished the meal in silence. Even Bonnie stopped pushing her food 'round and began to eat.

Two

By the time my friend Thrash and I got to school the next morning, it was still pretty early. Andrew's gang was already there. Sammy Minor and Mungo Hubbard and Mac Flemmons. Mac was already eating his lunch.

I knew they were going to start teasing me the minute I walked over to them. It looked like they started teasing me when they stopped teasing Thrash. I wasn't in any mood to let them get to me. I parked my bike, locked it, and headed for the building.

"Hi," I said when I'd reached the steps.

"Hey, where's Andrew?" Mungo asked.

"He's on his way, I guess," I said. I climbed two steps. I had to walk wide around Mac Flemmons 'cause he was built like a barrel and ate everything that wasn't glued down. He smiled as I passed.

After Mac finished chewing a big bite of apple, he said, "Alex, the paper boy. Curly-headed Alex." He tousled my hair.

"Watch it," I said.

"Your big-eye self," Mungo said.

"No teasing, it's too early."

They all started laughing. Then Sammy Minor said, "It's never too early for fun." I pushed past him and went into the building.

As the outer door closed behind me, before I got too far away I heard Mungo say, "Moon-eyes." They were still laughing when Thrash fell into step with me.

"You know, if you beat them up, you'll be all right. 'Member how they used to tease me?"

"Yeah. Is that what you did, beat them up?"

"Naw I scared them when they saw me going down to the Y every day after school. They thought I was learning judo or something."

"They just playing," I told Thrash. "I'll see you for lunch out under the big tree."

Thrash waved and turned the corner, heading to his room.

Andrew's gang was still out on the steps laughing it up. They laughed so loud it seemed like they rattled the glass in the double doors. My ears were hot. I walked faster and turned the corner, closing myself off from their teasing and laughing.

That's why I'd stopped going to the lot with

them. They always came by the house to play ball with Andrew and some of the neighborhood guys. I just left them alone, mostly, and they played with Andrew. I didn't like them teasing me like that. Teasing's all right, I guess. It's just that they didn't know when to let up. I never said a word about Mac being fat. I could've called him "bubblebutt." Other guys did. But I never called anybody anything except his name.

When the 2:50 bell rang, ending school for the day, I went to the rack to get my bike. I unlocked it from the rack and jumped on it and pedaled away as fast as the rusted old wheel would carry me.

In front of my house, I lay the bike on the ground 'cause it had no stand and ran into the house.

I slammed my books on the dining room table with a bang, went to the fridge, and got a can of Dr Pepper.

After I drank my pop, I squeezed the can into an aluminum ball and pitched it across the kitchen into the garbage can. "Good shot. Too bad Andrew didn't see that," I said, and raced up the stairs. I clomped on the stairs as noisily as Andrew did.

I slammed the door to my room and went straight to the closet. I lifted the loose bricks out of the back of the wall and took the plastic jar that I was using for a bank. The jar was heavy. I almost dropped it.

I poured the money out on my desk. I took out

10

a ten-dollar bill for paint. It was time to paint the old wheel. I'd been putting it off ever since that summer when I bought the bike from a boy across town for twelve dollars. He'd been in a hurry to sell 'cause he wanted to see a great new science fiction flick real bad. I thought the bike was worth more than twelve dollars. To me, it was.

And I had to take good care of it until I saved enough money to buy the one I really wanted. I glanced over at the mirror where I kept the clipping of the bike I wanted. That bike costed a lot of money, but it was worth it. I thought maybe I shouldn't even paint my old bike, 'cause at the rate I was going, I wouldn't have enough money for a long time.

I looked at the money still in the jar. I started to put the ten dollars back. But I didn't. Maybe my bike would last longer if I painted it. Hold down the rust some.

I looked at my watch. I'd have to hurry if I wanted to get to the hardware store after I delivered papers, I thought.

Stuffing the money into the pocket of my jeans, I got up, took the jar back to the closet.

Cement dust sifted down onto my gym shoes and onto the boxes on the floor of the closet as I put the jar back into its hiding place. I brushed at my clothes, making sure no dust was on them.

Going outside, I met Andrew. "Let me use your bike. You ain't gonna throw papers now, are you?"

he said, already grabbing my bike.

Before I could answer, he'd hopped on my bike and was halfway to the corner. I raced after him. "Andrew!" I shouted, but it was no use. He'd already turned the corner, pedaling like a bat out of hell.

I sat on the top step, my elbows on my knees, chin resting in my hands, waiting. I sat there a long time, even when the sun got low enough and started burning into my neck. I stayed there, waiting.

I looked at my watch. It was almost five o'clock. I couldn't wait for Andrew any longer. My customers were waiting for their papers.

I went through to the kitchen. Mama was at the sink, washing green beans. "I'm going to deliver my papers. I'll be late." I grabbed a celery stick out of a platter on the counter and bit into it. "See you, Mama," I said, rushing out the door.

"Be careful," she said after me. "Wait. Alex, why will you be late?"

"Andrew has my bike again."

"I'm going to talk to him soon as I get him in here," Mama said.

Still chewing on celery, I walked the two blocks to the bus stop. "Delivering papers on the bus," I muttered as I dipped into my pocket for a dollar and a quarter.

I climbed on the bus and paid my fare. I went all the way to the back of the bus. The bus was almost empty. My neighborhood is near the end of the line, and there wouldn't be a lot of riders until the bus was almost downtown, where I had to transfer to another bus.

I sat in a corner seat, leaned against the window, using my canvas sack for a pillow. As long as it takes to get downtown, I could've taken a nap, only I couldn't. I kept thinking about Andrew. What did he need my bike for? Why didn't he come right back like he said? I know for Andrew, "right back" means two days later, but he could've kept his promise. I hoped he didn't let anything happen to my bike.

I couldn't buy paint for my bike 'cause I didn't get through throwing papers until almost 7:30. By then, it was too late to do anything, 'cause even if the hardware store was still open, by the time I took the long bus ride home, it would've been too dark to paint it.

It was late that night when Andrew came home. So late that I would've been asleep, only I couldn't sleep for worrying what could've happened to my bike.

"You still woke?" Andrew said.

"Yeah. My bike's all right?"

"Yeah. It's in the garage. It won't get wet or stolen."

"Andrew, please leave it alone."

He didn't answer me. All he said was, "Now you can go to sleep."

"No, I can't. It's way too hot."

I threw back the sheet and sat on the side of the bed. I searched the floor without looking until I found my slippers. I slipped my feet into them and got up. I got my robe off the back of a straight chair and pulled it on.

"Where you going?"

"Outside to check my bike." I moved toward the door. It looked like Andrew wanted to say something but didn't. It was so quiet I could hear the breeze stirring the leaves on the big tree 'round back.

Finally, he said, "It must be raining out there." He went down the hall to the bathroom and started filling the tub.

I sat on the side of the bed, feeling real hot. The wind was blowing good and cool through the open window, and then I felt a few drops of rain. But I didn't get up and shut the window. I lay back on the pillow and put my hands under my head. "I'm gonna have to keep Andrew away from my bike," I said.

I got up, pulled off my robe and slippers, then lay back down again.

Three

Andrew came out of the bathroom, rubbing his hair with a big blue towel. He had on pajamas with the jacket open. He crossed to the dresser and went on toweling his hair. He looked into the mirror, smiling and cocking his head to the side as he wiped.

"Andrew, where did you go?"

He didn't answer. He draped the towel 'round his neck and combed his hair. He started whistling. I wasn't in the mood to hear him whistle. I still couldn't go to sleep because of the heat. I got up.

I had to step over Andrew's clothes where he'd left a trail of them on the way to the bathroom. "You'd better put your clothes in the dirty clothes hamper," I said. I warned him 'cause I didn't want

Mama to holler at him, especially since I was getting ready to yell at him myself.

"I'll get them in the morning before I go to school."

"I think you should get them now. So Mama won't start screaming. And wake Bonnie."

"I better go see 'bout the little baby. She must've missed her big brother today."

"Don't go in there," I said, feeling real brave.

"Huh?" His eyes got big as saucers. His mouth dropped open like a drawbridge in front of a castle.

"You heard me."

As he started down the hall, he said, "Some folks get riled up over one little rusty bike."

I was standing only a few feet away from Andrew. I grabbed him 'round the neck without hesitating at all. I started squeezing. He's bigger than me and shook me off easily. I hit the floor like a sack of potatoes. My head bumped the edge of the door. I raised up to a sitting position and held my head. But I couldn't stop the pain.

Andrew bent over me. Looking directly at me, he said, "Your bike's in the garage. There's nothing wrong with it that wasn't wrong with it before I borrowed it. Get that through your thick skull. Hear?"

The pain in my head eased up some. I felt the lump on the back of my head to see if it was bleeding. It wasn't.

Andrew stood in the doorway like he wasn't

scared of anything in the world. I wasn't scared anymore. I knew he could beat me, but I had to try to defend myself.

"You great big old ape," I said.

"Yeah?"

"Yeah," I said. "You gonna leave my bike alone. I never would've borrowed your bike and went 'round talking 'bout it like you doing."

Andrew stood in the doorway. He licked his lips, his tongue darting out over his fat brown mouth. We were so quiet, I thought he could hear my heart pounding against my ribs. I grabbed him 'round the waist and tried to pull him down. It was like tugging at a wall. He put his hands on my shoulders and lifted me up. He flipped me 'round until he had one hand on my chest and the other on my left leg. He threw me on top of his bed as if I weighed three pounds. When I hit the bed, the box springs and mattress crashed to the floor. The bookcase headboard fell over on me, sending books and the little crystal-clear vase crashing to the floor.

I flailed my arms about, throwing books off me, trying to get up. I think a dictionary hit Andrew. He threw it back. "You ain't had enough?" he said. I threw more books on the floor trying to get free.

"You gonna clean up this mess before Mama think I did it?"

"It's your bed," I told him.

I was finally able to pull myself out of the wreckage and stumble to my feet. I pulled my pajamas up and buttoned my jacket. While I was buttoning my jacket, Andrew grabbed me 'round the neck and threw me on the floor, away from the beds. "I'm gonna sleep in your bed, if you ain't gonna fix mine."

"You can sleep on the roof. Pitch a tent in the backyard. You ain't sharing my bed with me. I shared my bike."

"Who said anything about sharing?"

By then, I was fighting mad. I picked myself up to a sitting position and grabbed Andrew 'round the ankles. Before he realized what'd happened, I had him down on the floor. He let out a grunt. I sat astraddle his chest, with all my weight. I wasn't going to get up unless dynamite blasted me up.

"OFF-F-F-F-F," Andrew moaned.

I had to stay on top of him or he'd get up and twist my arm till it popped. And I didn't want my arm to pop. That was one of Andrew's favorite things to do to somebody when he had them down.

From on top of Andrew's chest, I got a good look at the room. It was a real mess even before we broke the bed. Andrew's clothes were thrown about as if it'd been raining boys' clothing. He didn't keep any of his sports equipment in the closet like he should've. There was a soccer ball, basketball, and a football over in the corner. They looked like weird, colored grapefruits. Clothing

18

was half-in and half-out of his chest of drawers. I sure hope Mama don't see this mess, I thought as I eased off Andrew.

"AEEEIIEEE!" I was too late. Mama stood in the doorway, her hands on her hips. She didn't say anything else. She just stood there, trembling. Finally, she said, "I see you-all been fighting again. Get up right now. Both of you. And clean this room. And don't make any more noise and wake Bonnie."

Mama turned, started out.

Andrew said real low, hardly more than a whisper, "If Bonnie slept through that scream, she'll sleep through anything."

"What? I don't want any sass from you, young man," she said to Andrew. She flounced out of the room. Just outside the doorway, she stopped and said, "I'll be back to check it before I go to bed."

I stood at the dresser, watching Andrew look over the mess. I admit I did throw 'round a lot of books when we were fighting, but most of the mess was Andrew's. Ever since I moved into his room, he didn't give me but a little space. I was just his little brother, forced to share rooms with him. I kept the little area he gave me pretty clean. I'd had a perfectly good room of my own until Bonnie was born. Giving my room up to Bonnie didn't make me mad — not much anyway. I still liked her, but Andrew got real mad about this.

Daddy had to come and holler at Andrew. And I don't think Andrew ever really got over it.

"Ain't you gonna help?" Andrew was saying.

"Yeah. Soon's you promise to keep away from my bike."

"I might need to borrow it again. Sometime soon."

"Well, I guess I'll just stretch out here on my bed and feel the cool breeze blow in through the window. Turn out the light when you finish, okay?" I grinned and turned over away from him.

"You could help me fix the bed back. It's a two-man job."

"I'll help you soon's you get the mess cleaned off the floor." I turned back to look at him.

Andrew pursed his lips and halfheartedly bent down and picked two books off the floor. He threw them on top of my desk. They struck the goldfish bowl, and my two fish sloshed 'round in the clear water. They raced 'round and 'round like in a relay. "You made my fish dizzy."

"You oughta help me." He bent down again and scooped an armful of clothing off the floor. He went to the closet, kicked the door open wider with his right foot, and tossed the clothes inside. The other things in his closet had been placed none too fussily, and with this new bundle, the inside of the closet looked a little bit worse than the city dump. At least some of the trash at the city dump was stacked pretty neat.

When he'd finished clearing off the floor, I got

up and helped him fix the bed. I looked 'round the room. It wasn't half bad. It wasn't the greatest, either.

Later, true to her word, Mama came back and checked the room. "It'll have to do till morning. Although it isn't the finest room I've seen." She'd brought Daddy with her. He looked 'round the room, but I couldn't tell what his expression said. He kind of smiled-winced, like he did when something'd upset his stomach.

But when they turned 'round to leave, I could tell by the way Daddy pulled down on the light switch that the room wasn't suitable to him. I guess he would've paddled us if the schools still allowed paddling. I think Daddy stopped paddling us when he learned he couldn't paddle his students anymore. Not that music students were likely to need much paddling. But Daddy just grabbed at the light switch like he was gonna tear it off the wall. In the darkness, I heard the door closing.

Four

About three times a week, somebody has to go out at 2:30 and clean erasers. Lately, it has been me. It got so Mrs. Reid didn't have to call on me. She'd hold up an eraser, nod at me, and I knew to get on the job.

I walked along the aisle between the last rows of seats and the window. All of the windows were open on account of the heat. I looked out of the window in time to see Andrew.

He was picking the lock on the chain that held my bike in the rack. I gathered up an armload of erasers and hurried out.

I was too late.

When I got outside, Andrew was pedaling across the school ground. Before I even had a chance to yell at him, he disappeared up MacFarland Avenue, heading east.

I sat on the steps and halfheartedly knocked the erasers on the cement. What I really wished was that I was knocking Andrew's head on the steps.

Between erasers, I glanced at my watch. Time was dragging. When you're pounding erasers, you don't really have to watch what you're doing. Just keep pounding them on the steps. So I pounded erasers and watched across the school ground.

But Andrew did not come back.

I went on hoping he'd show up by 2:50. I didn't want to finish the erasers and go back inside knowing my bike was missing.

I looked over at the bike rack. There were lots of bikes there, including Thrash's. But there was just a gaping hole where mine should've been. I looked at the space that used to hold my bike. That's when I saw a piece of paper fluttering in the wind. I put the two erasers I'd been beating down on the step and went over. The paper was held down by the bottom of a broken pop bottle. I picked it up.

Andrew's note said: *I'll leave your bike in the garage. See you. A.W., Jr.*

I crumpled the note, threw it on the ground, and went back to my erasers.

It's sad to say that when I got home, my bike wasn't in the garage like Andrew'd promised. It wasn't 'round back, either. I didn't know where it was. All I knew was that the sun was getting hotter and papers were waiting to be delivered.

I went 'round to the front of the house and sat on the steps, waiting. Although I'd given up hope that Andrew'd come back soon, I went on waiting. Something was up. He'd never borrowed my bike from school like that before. And, why wasn't he in his classes? What was wrong with Andrew, I wondered. After one more glance up the street, I left to throw papers.

It was almost 7:30 when I got through delivering papers. It wasn't dark because of daylight savings time, but even if I wanted to play football with Andrew — which I didn't — there wouldn't be enough time. I had too much homework. Good thing I wanted to pass on into the next grade. Andrew'd been held back before, and I sure didn't want to stay in the sixth grade another year. By the time I got to high school, I was gonna have a new bike to ride. A brand-new one, still in the carton, that I'd have to put together myself.

But I needed my old beat-up bike now. I needed it more than ever. So I wouldn't have to take all afternoon with the papers. Or spend my money as fast as I made it for bus fare.

I was sweating when I got to Mrs. Pettaway's yard. I wiped my face. That didn't help much. I trekked 'cross her neatly cut yard and climbed up on her porch. It was supposed to be a short cut, but it didn't seem like one to me. I had Mrs. Pettaway's paper in my hand, rolled into a tomahawk. I was hoping I could slam the paper against her screen door like I did the other day and go on home, but as soon as I got to her porch, she stuck her head out of the door.

"HEY! ALEX! GOT AN EXTRA?!" She always yelled loud 'cause she was hard of hearing and thought everybody else was, too, I guess.

"YES, MA'AM!" I hollered back just as loud. I handed her the paper. She gripped it in her bony fingers.

"If you got a minute, read me a few headlines," she said in a softer voice since I was so much closer to her.

I sat on the porch swing. She sat in the glider, rocking it gently so it wouldn't squeak loud. I opened out the paper and began to read. She always found one article for me to read all the way through. I don't know how she knew, but it was usually the longest article in the paper. So there I was, almost shouting sentences at Mrs. Pettaway, when Andrew and his hoodlums came by.

They usually took a break at the soda fountain at Shepard's Pharmacy, then went back to playing. If none of them had any money, they took a break at our refrigerator.

"READ THAT A LITTLE LOUDER, WILL YOU?" Mrs. Pettaway said as soon as Andrew and his pack got in front of her house.

Andrew didn't slow down. He stuck his tongue

out at me and kept right on walking, Mungo and Mac behind him. Andrew pointed to the garage and went on into the house. He'd given me a look that said, "I'm glad you're up there and not me." Then he went on into the house to raid the fridge.

I wasn't so lucky with his little pals. They were flashing their teeth before they even got to Mrs. Pettaway's. They were keeping in step like twin boys or marchers in a parade.

"Look at old big-eye Alex," Mungo said.

"He can see the whole page at one time with them big old eyes," Mac put in.

I wanted to yell back at them: "I bet I ain't no old dummy or fat" but I just kept my eyes on the newspaper. Then, when they started laughing, I could've rammed the newspaper down their throats. But what I did was turn the page.

Mungo and Mac went into my house while I finished up the article I was reading. My throat was dry and scratchy, and I needed a cold drink. But I knew to wait until they came out.

I shook the newspaper out, trying to make it neat. I folded it as fast as I could before Mrs. Pettaway got a chance to say something mushy, like how sweet I was to read the paper to a ninety-nine-year-old woman.

I handed her the paper and stood up and stretched. I'd cooled off a bit from sitting on her shady porch, but I was still tired.

She took the paper and tucked it under her arm.

"I'm gonna put this in the box with my others. That was a real good article you read."

I grinned without answering and started down the steps, my knees popping as I walked.

I met Mungo and Mac going back to the field. Each was carrying a sweating can of pop. I hope there's some left, I thought, going into the house.

Andrew was still in the kitchen. He had one long arm against the refrigerator door, the other turned a can of pop up until he'd drained it.

"Where's my bike?"

"In the garage where it's s'posed to be." He set the empty can on the table.

"Don't touch it again."

"What you gonna do?"

"Try it and see."

I went out the back door and on 'round to the garage. My bike was there all right. It was propped against the garage wall. Just as rusty as before. Just as beautiful as before.

I stood looking at it, wanting to find something wrong with it. But it was just as sharp as it was before Andrew'd borrowed it.

I left the bike in the garage and went upstairs to do my homework. I wondered why Andrew hadn't been in school the whole day. I wondered where he'd gone, what he'd done.

But by the time I was sitting to my desk and attacking the long division, I'd forgotten everything. Especially how to work long division problems.

Five

The next morning, I got up a little earlier and checked over my long division problems. They were all right, I guess. Anyway they were neat. I hadn't erased too much. Mrs. Reid was always taking off points for sloppy work. I closed my notebook and got ready for school.

Andrew was turned over on his side. I started to wake him up but didn't. I gathered up my books and carried them downstairs to the living room. I could already smell bacon and toast and grits.

"You're up early this morning," Daddy said.

"I couldn't sleep. I had trouble with my bike and with my arithmetic homework." I sat to the table and Mama gave me breakfast.

"I hope you're hungry," she said.

I wasn't hungry, but I didn't say anything. It

looked like Mama'd gone to a lot of trouble. At the stove, she poured herself a cup of coffee, then came to the table and sat down.

"What's with Andrew and your bicycle?" she asked. "Where does he go when he borrows it?"

"I don't know. I guess he's just mean to me."

"Nonsense." She sipped her coffee. "I don't think he'd be out and out mean to you."

"I don't care how mean he is to me, I just want him to leave my bike alone. I don't even know what he's doing with it. I'm trying to save money for a new bike, but I won't be able to do it if he's gonna keep on taking my old bike."

I gulped down my orange juice and pushed my plate aside. I scraped back my chair and stood up. "I'm going to school."

I went upstairs and brushed my teeth. I beat Andrew into the bathroom by only a few seconds. If he'd been faster or wide awake, I never would've got in there first.

When I came out, he was standing outside the door, swaying like he was still fast asleep. I grinned at him and went back downstairs.

I got my books off the lamp table in the living room and started out. " 'Bye, Mama and Daddy," I said.

The storm door hissed shut as I went out.

By the time I got to Thrash Peabody's house, he and his mother were still eating breakfast. His mother was getting ready to leave for work at the hospital. Mrs. Peabody was dressed in all white. On the pocket of her lab jacket was a gold pin that said, CARLA PEABODY, R.N.

"Want some juice, Alex? Some toast?" Mrs. Peabody asked.

"No, ma'am," I said. "I've just finished breakfast. Thanks anyhow."

"Sit down. A little juice never hurt anybody." She got a glass out of the cupboard and poured me orange juice from a carton on the table.

I put my lunch and books on an empty chair and sat at the table with the Peabodys. Sometimes, I came over and worked out with Thrash's bodybuilding equipment. He was always trying to build up his body. You'd never know it to look at Thrash, though. He was as skinny as a stick of spaghetti. But not nearly as skinny as Mungo Hubbard. Daddy said it was more important to build up your self-confidence than to develop muscles. Anyway, Thrash was taller than me, and he wore glasses as thick as pop bottle bottoms. They made his eyes look big — big as eggs, even bigger than mine.

Mrs. Peabody pushed back her chair and stood. "I better go. Lock up, son." She took another sip of her coffee and set the cup in the sink. She took her shoulder purse off the back of a chair, started out.

At the door, she turned and said, "Thrasher, I

almost forgot. I saw them first thing this morning. Get the bugs out of my refrigerator. Take them up to your room where I can't see them."

"Aw, Ma, they'll dry out."

"Get them out of my refrigerator. It is not a morgue."

"I gotta keep 'em on ice. I need 'em for a science project."

"Not in my refrigerator with my food."

After Mrs. Peabody left, I told Thrash, "Put some ice cubes in your picnic cooler and keep the bugs there until your class is over." I was glad I didn't have science with Thrash. My teacher was still on astronomy, my favorite.

While he washed breakfast dishes, I began filling the cooler with ice from the ice maker in their refrigerator. I let Thrash take the bugs out of the fridge.

He kept the bugs in little jars. Except the tarantula. It was in a bigger jar 'cause it was the biggest and hairiest tarantula I ever saw outside of the movies. Thrash also had bees, fireflies, a cockroach, and a monarch butterfly.

I hope my class never studies whatever Thrash was studying. We could stay on astronomy until I graduated high school for all I cared. His mother only hollered at him. My mother would've flipped all the way out if I brought bugs into the house. Dead or alive.

"Alex, what happened to you yesterday? I stopped by to see you, but you were gone. Still throwing papers?"

"I had to deliver papers on the bus. Well, not really on the bus. I had to ride the bus to my route. Then I had to walk. Andrew didn't come back with my bike. No matter what I do, he seems to keep my bike longer than he should." I laughed.

Thrash pushed up his glasses. He looked at his watch, pushed up his glasses some more. "We better get going or we'll be late."

He gathered up his books, leafed through them to make sure he hadn't forgotten anything. "If it was me, know what I'd do?"

"No. What?" I said, following him out. He locked the door, checked to make sure it was locked.

"Booby-trap it," Thrash said. "Take the wheels off it, see if he'd put them back on again." Thrash laughed. I did, too, because I couldn't see Andrew fixing my bike. Unless, I thought, he needed it desperately. Maybe what Thrash said wasn't such a bad idea.

"Riding the bus must be something," Thrash was saying.

"It is."

We were almost at school, about a block away, when Thrash said, "I wish I had a brother or sister. You sure are lucky. You got Andrew *and* Bonnie."

"I don't know if I'm lucky or not. With your older brother, you get beat up. He takes all your things. And you get to baby-sit your sister." I thought again about how Andrew'd had a fit when Daddy moved me into Andrew's room. Maybe Andrew didn't like having a little sister and a little brother, either. I didn't wanna give Bonnie my room, but she had to sleep somewhere.

When I got to school, I saw Ellis Murdock sitting on the steps with Sammy Minor. They were bouncing a ball back and forth between them.

"Teacher's pet," Ellis said to me. "I almost sat down in some of your eraser dust." He was clutching a brown bag lunch in one hand, but he didn't miss a single bounce.

I went up the steps not caring if the ball hit me or not. Thrash was right behind me.

When I turned down the hallway, Mac Flemmons was waiting at the door to my classroom. He was eating his lunch. Most of the guys who hung around with Andrew were still going to elementary school. Andrew would've been, too, but when he got held back last time, he got some bleach and erased what the teacher'd written on his report card. Using Daddy's fountain pen, he changed his card to read, *Promoted to Grade Seven.* I knew Andrew was wrong, but nobody ever said anything to him about it.

Andrew still didn't study. If he didn't pass from seventh grade, I'd catch up with him. Some guys, like Ellis, got held back two times. In Ellis's case, if he could get graded for lunch, he'd have the best report card in the whole school.

"Pass your homework assignments to the front," Mrs. Reid said when we were seated. "Alex, I want you to go to the supply room and get a box of chalk. I have some hard problems to put on the board."

A voice in the back of the room said: "Is there any other kind?"

The class snickered.

"First, let me call the roll." Mrs. Reid got her book and pen and said, "Adams, Babcock, Murphy, Lewis, Murdock — "

"Present," Ellis said.

Slowly, the door was being opened. A head poked in but did not come all the way into the room.

Mrs. Reid said, "Jackson, Gray, Minor, Hubbard?" She looked across to Mungo's empty seat, shook her head, and scribbled something in her book. I started for the supply room as she said, "And Alexander Walker."

"Boy! Are you late," I said as I got to the door where Mungo was still trying to sneak in.

"I got held up by a freight train," he said. "Look, Alex, go back into the room. If I can sneak in behind you, old Reid'll mark me on time."

"You too late for that," I said. "Old Reid — as you call her — has already taken roll."

"Try it anyway," Mungo begged. "If Reid marks me late again, she might call my father. He'll have a fit."

"You're too tall," I said, and went on down the hall to the supply room.

When I got back with the chalk, Mungo bent down as low as he could and tried to follow me into the classroom. I knew it wouldn't work. Mrs. Reid was busy somewhere else, but she'd have to be blind to miss Mungo. And she didn't.

"Well, Mr. Hubbard. I see we started class a bit too early for you today."

Mungo straightened and twisted his mouth into an embarrassed grin. "No, ma'am."

"I suppose you have a note for being late."

"No, ma'am."

"March right to your seat and write, 'I will not be late for school,' one hundred times."

I gave Mrs. Reid the box of chalk. She opened it, took out a long stick, and broke it in half. She went to the board. "This is for those students interested in learning. And I hope that's all of you. Write a composition on the following topic."

On the board, she'd written: THE SICKEST I'VE EVER BEEN.

"It's due first thing Monday morning." She placed the stick of chalk in the tray at the bottom of the blackboard. She rubbed her hands together to get rid of chalk dust. "Now that everyone has copied that, we'll read a chapter or two. I won't forget the problems."

Things went smoothly until lunchtime. I don't think Mungo liked having to write all those sentences, but he did have until Monday to finish them. Anyway, it meant he'd probably have to stay away from the lot.

As soon as the bell rang at the beginning of lunch period, I grabbed my lunch and went out and sat under a big shady tree. I didn't see Thrash. We usually ate lunch together. I peeled wax paper off my bologna sandwich and was getting ready to take a bite. But before I could, Mungo came dashing over to me. He was already tall and thin, but he was taking long steps like a grown man. And he looked mad.

I don't know Mungo's real name. Everyone — even teachers — called him Mungo. I couldn't believe he had a birth certificate somewhere that said Mungo Hubbard. I bet his real name is something even weirder than Alexander Osgood Walker. Or it might be something simple like Richard. Richard is Thrash's real first name. Anyway, I'll ask Mungo what his real name is when he's in a better mood, I decided.

Mungo bent low and sat on the grass in front of me. "I been looking all over for you," he said.

I didn't say anything. I took a sip of milk and bit into my sandwich. I squinted over at Mungo. The sun was hot and bright even under the tree like that. I went on eating.

"If you had hid me better, I wouldn't be in trouble with old lady Reid."

"Huh?"

"You could've sneaked me into Reid's class," Mungo went on.

"Boy, what's wrong with you?"

"Nothing," Mungo said, standing. "A lot of something's gonna be wrong with you when I get through with you."

"I didn't make you late," I said. "Besides, didn't you hear her taking roll when you were standing in the door?"

It was like he hadn't heard a word I said. "I don't like big-mouthed people." He turned real fast and started off. Slowing, he turned, and wagged a finger at me. "I want you to write my sentences for me. And my essay, too. Or else." He flounced away without waiting for me to reply.

I finished my lunch and spent the rest of the period in the library, reading magazines. I wasn't scared of Mungo Hubbard or anybody else. He was just bigger than me, that's all. The bigger they are, the harder they fall, I hoped.

The bell rang. I got up and went to my classroom.

I couldn't remember a single magazine I'd skimmed through in the library.

Six

After school, I went home and tossed my books on top of my desk. One of them slid off the stack onto the floor, but I didn't care.

If Mungo thought I was gonna take his punishment for him, he was not only bean-pole skinny, but crazy as a loon.

I went back outside, hopped on my bike, and pedaled away. I would go deliver my papers first. Sometimes they were at the drop point early, sometimes they weren't. If they weren't there, I'd wait for them.

When I got to the corner in the development where my papers were, I stopped and looked at the houses. They were all new. Or, at least, looked new. Like houses in a magazine. Houses you just dream exist. And my papers were on the corner where they should have been. They were wrapped over with a piece of newspaper and tied so the wind wouldn't blow them away.

I untied the bundled papers and folded the papers into tomahawks so they'd fit into my canvas sack. Tomahawks always made the papers seem lighter. They sure were easier to handle.

The first customer on my route was Mrs. Kirkland. She was kind of fussy. I had to put her paper in the long red mailbox on the side of the red door. Her whole house was trimmed in red. Anytime I missed putting her paper in the red mailbox, she'd dart from 'round the side of her house.

"Alex," she'd say. "Put it in the mailbox. Not on the mat. And don't throw it and hit the door and scratch the paint. The other boy didn't care where he put it. One time, we even had to get it off the roof."

I wanted to please all my customers as well as I could. Especially Mrs. Kirkland. She'd given me a ten-dollar tip at Christmas. It was a check. She made it payable to Alexander Walker. I liked that. She'd remembered my name.

When I'd finished all the papers but one, I climbed back on my bike and pedaled to the shopping center. I stopped at the newsstand to look over the comic books.

I bought two comic books, then left the store. They were so interesting, I was still leafing through them at the corner while waiting for the light to change. That's when I saw Mungo Hubbard.

He was leaning against a streetlight post and licking an ice-cream cone. "Where's my sentences, boy?" he asked, barely stopping with his licking. He had his shirt sleeves rolled up to the shoulder to show off muscles he didn't have.

"Hi," I said. The light'd changed, and I was getting ready to go. I tossed the comic books into the bag with Mrs. Pettaway's paper.

Mungo stopped licking his ice cream long enough to say, "I can't beat you up now, but you better have those sentences ready by Monday morning. Time running out."

I pedaled on up the street and looked back in time to see Mungo shake a fist at me.

I went through the back way and in through the kitchen where Mama was putting the finishing touches on supper. She smiled when she saw me. "Wash up, Alex. Dinner's almost ready."

"Yes, ma'am," I said. I remembered Mrs. Pettaway's paper. I went out through the front of the house and across the yard. I quietly tucked Mrs. Pettaway's paper inside her screen door.

Our storm door hissed shut behind me as I ran upstairs and into the bathroom to wash up.

After I came out of the bathroom, I peeped into Bonnie's room. She was in her playpen and, I guess, resting before dinner. A breeze blew in through the thin curtains at her window. It was cool in her room. I took her out of the playpen and carried her downstairs with me.

Downstairs, Daddy was standing in the doorway, looking out. He held the evening paper in one hand. "Hello," he said, when he saw Bonnie and me. He tweaked Bonnie's nose.

I took Bonnie into the kitchen and put her in her high chair.

From the kitchen, I heard Daddy yell for Andrew. He never had to call Andrew twice. Then Daddy said, "Alex! This newspaper is pretty badly printed. Do you have an extra?"

"No, sir." I went into the living room. Daddy held the paper open so I could see it. A whole page was blank, streaked with black where words should've been.

"All of them are probably like that anyhow," Daddy said.

I looked out the door and saw Andrew bouncing across the street, his T-shirt hanging out of his jeans. It was still clean and white where it'd been tucked inside his jeans.

Sweating and gasping for breath, Andrew stood in the doorway. He lifted the front of his T-shirt and wiped his face. His white hightop leather gym shoes were caked with red dirt. He stamped his feet and dust flew about.

"Hi," he said, grinning.

"Andrew," Daddy said. He shook out the paper as if he was going to read it, then took a long look at Andrew. "Boy, you are a mess. Before you go to the table, wash up. No. You take a whole tub bath. And don't be too late for dinner."

"Aw, okay," Andrew said. He bounded up the stairs, taking them two at a time. They creaked like they were gonna break off and fall into the cellar.

"Andrew, come back here."

The stairs creaked. Andrew came back down. "Sir?"

"Wipe that grin off your face." Andrew stopped grinning. "Now. You turn around and walk up the stairs like the bathroom isn't going to run away before you get there."

His head down, shoulders back, Andrew went up the stairs.

A short time later, Andrew came downstairs looking like a new boy. He had on a clean shirt and there wasn't any grit on his fingers. He wore his school shoes. He took his seat at the table. Bonnie was in her high chair next to him. He leaned over toward Bonnie.

"Give me a kiss, Bon," he said.

Bonnie kissed him. She smiled. Andrew put a finger in the corner of his mouth and stretched his mouth as wide as he could. He stuck his tongue out and wiggled it at Bonnie. She grinned. He rolled his eyes from side to side until only the whites were showing. Bonnie giggled.

Mama and Daddy seated themselves. And after Andrew stopped playing with Bonnie, he reached for a large slab of fried fish. He had the fish on his plate and a piece in his mouth when Daddy said, "Say grace, Andrew."

He chewed the fish in his mouth and swallowed, staring at Daddy all the time. "Huh?"

"I think I said it very distinctly," Daddy told him.

"Aw — all right," Andrew said, twisting in his chair. He bowed his head.

I bowed my head, too, but kept an eye on Andrew. I kinda hoped he'd slip and say: "Good bread, good meat. Good gosh, let's eat." He always said that when he, Bonnie, and I ate by ourselves on days when Mama and Daddy weren't there. Instead, he said a pretty good grace.

I closed my eyes as Andrew said, "We give thanks for this food we are about to receive. It has been a very good day and we are grateful to You for it, God. Thank You for allowing us to be together at this most bountiful meal. In Jesus Christ's name, thank You, Amen."

When he finished saying grace, he looked at me and stuck out his tongue. If I hadn't seen it and heard it, I wouldn't have believed it.

I stared down at my empty plate. Was that Andrew? My brother, Andrew? I wanted him to mess up so Daddy'd beat him, and Mama'd make him wash dishes a whole week in a row. But Mama sat there smiling like someone'd told her she'd just won first prize in a raffle or something. If I

43

thought Mama was proud, Daddy's smile stretched from ear to ear like a jack-o'-lantern.

Daddy picked up the platter of fish and put some on his plate. He put some on Mama's plate, then handed it to me. He was still grinning, real silly-like.

I selected a piece of fish. By this time, even Bonnie was grinning, so I had to grin myself. Maybe old Andrew was gonna change. I hope.

Seven

But Andrew didn't change. At least, not then. Or the next day, either.

It was Saturday, but I got up early to paint my bike. It was a bright morning, kind of cloudy. I didn't want it to rain. I got all my supplies: a can of royal blue paint, thinner, brushes, and a bunch of old rags. I'd bought the paint and stuff at the hardware store on the corner.

I spread some newspapers on the driveway so I wouldn't splatter paint about. The sun peeped out from behind a cloud. The paint sparkled. It was a good day for painting, if it didn't rain.

I got busy, making up for lost time. I was so lost in stirring the paint, making sure it was just right, that at first, I didn't see Thrash come into the yard. He was like a shadow in the corner of my eye.

"So, you gonna paint the wheel," he said.

"Yeah. Finally," I answered.

"I hope it doesn't rain," Thrash said, looking at the sky. I looked, too. A big black cloud pushed in front of the sun. If I hurried, maybe I could get through before it rained.

I turned on the hose and squirted the wheel real nice. After I got through washing it, Thrash grabbed a handful of rags and helped me dry it off. It looked shiny with just a good washing.

If I went on and got the job done, I could probably ride the bike to throw papers that same afternoon.

A wind came up, fluttering the newspaper on the drive. I looked 'round for something to hold the edges down. In the garage, me and Thrash found a stack of bricks in a corner. We each grabbed three bricks, took them outside. But by then it'd already started raining. Big drops at first, then it slowed down a bit. Me and Thrash ran into the garage where we watched the rain.

I ran back out of the garage, got my bike, pushed it in. We stood in the garage, waiting, but it didn't look like the rain was gonna quit soon.

I went and put the lid on the can of paint and set it near the door of the garage. Thrash brought in the quart can of thinner.

By the time I'd picked up the soggy newspapers,

balled it up, and put it in the garbage can at the side of the garage, the rain speeded up again. "Come on, Thrash," I yelled.

He and I made a mad dash for the house.

It was too dark to paint inside the garage. There was nothing to do now except ride an unpainted bike another day.

When we got into the kitchen, Andrew was up. He was eating breakfast — cold cereal and bananas. He reached for the carton of milk in the center of the table and poured more milk on his cereal. He still looked sleepy.

"Where you two been?" he asked.

"I was going to paint my bike, but it started raining. Guess I'll do it tomorrow," I said. To Thrash, I said, "Sit down."

Without asking if Thrash was hungry, I got two bowls out of the cupboard, filled them with cereal. All the activity and disappointment made me hungry. Thrash poured milk on his cereal and started to dig in, pushing up his glasses at the same time.

After I'd eaten my cereal, the rain started even harder than before. It pounded on the kitchen window. And once, a big puddle poured under the bottom of the kitchen door.

I would have to mop the puddle later. I suddenly remembered my bike catalog. "Thrash, I got something you gotta see. It came in the mail yesterday." I scraped back my chair and raced upstairs.

The old staircase creaked real bad as I ran back down again. I had the catalog in my hand. The pages were slick and glossy, but some of them were already curled over where I'd looked through it a hundred times since I got it. I kept comparing it to the bike pictures I kept on the mirror. They were the same bikes.

Andrew finished his cereal. When I went into the kitchen, he stood, stretched, but he still looked sleepy. "You got dishes, little brother," he said. He patted me on the head as he went out. He was almost to the living room door, but he came back, picked up his dishes, and put them into the sink.

While Thrash was looking through the bike catalog, I washed dishes and cleaned off the table. All the dishes we used today, I had to wash. I glanced at the calendar to make sure. Andrew kept the calendar hanging behind the kitchen door, clearly marked, so he wouldn't wash dishes on my day by mistake. To him, that would've been worse than anything, even missing a game out in the lot. So that we wouldn't get our names mixed up, he wrote AOW for me and AW for him. Tomorrow — Sunday — was Andrew's day. I didn't envy him. We'd have a big meal, lots of dishes. I hoped Mama was planning on company so there'd be even more dishes. I grinned, thinking about him cleaning up on Sunday.

"Whew!" I said, as I hung the dish towel on the rack. "This is hard work."

"What do you mean, hard work? I wash dishes almost everyday." Thrash said, looking up from the catalog. "My mother only washes them on her days off. But I guess she's tired from working all day."

Maybe it wasn't so bad having to wash dishes every other day. "You do need a sister or a brother," I told Thrash. "Let's go upstairs, Thrash. After I pick out my bike, I want to show you my new space comic book."

When we got upstairs, Andrew was lying on his unmade bed. His half of the room was a mess. I pulled Andrew's desk chair over to my desk so Thrash could sit while we looked through the catalog.

Thrash sat down, placed the catalog opened in front of me. "Look, this is the greatest bike in the catalog." Thrash said, grinning. He pushed up his glasses, still grinning.

I studied it, found its price in the listing. "It should be the greatest bike in the world for that price. Three hundred and fifty dollars. It's a pretty color, though. Turn toward the back. Those are more in my price range."

Thrash flipped pages, pushed up his glasses.

I said, "The blue one. It's the same color I want to paint my old bike."

"One-oh-nine, ninety-five. Good price," Thrash said, as if he knew everything about bikes.

"The way I figure it, maybe I can save that

much money by the time I get to high school or something."

"It sure is neat," Thrash said.

Over on his bed, Andrew'd gone back to sleep. He was snoring like he was sawing logs. I looked back at him and laughed. Thrash laughed, too.

We were quiet for a while. The rain had slacked up. The only sound was Andrew sawing logs.

Finally, Thrash said, "Are you gonna order this bike?"

"I don't know. I might just look 'round in the stores downtown first."

"Good idea. You'd get it faster."

I got up, went to the bookcase by the door. I took a comic book off the stack on top of the bookcase and brought it over to Thrash. "Did you read this?"

"No. Can I take it home with me?"

"Yeah."

Thrash got up, went to the window. He pulled the curtains back, looked out. "I think the rain's stopped. I better go home," he said. He started downstairs. I went with him to the door and on downstairs.

At the door, he opened it, stepped through. "See you," he said.

"See you." By the time the storm door hissed shut, I was in the kitchen mopping up the puddle by the door.

Eight

After I'd mopped up the puddle, I leafed through the catalog again, but I already knew exactly which bicycle I'd buy. I closed the catalog, opened a drawer, dropped the catalog into it, and slammed the drawer shut again.

I went to my bed and lay down, reading a space comic book I'd already read a hundred times. Andrew'd turned over on his side and had stopped snoring.

I stayed on the bed, looking through the comic book. I wasn't really reading 'cause I already knew it by heart, probably.

Around three o'clock, Andrew got up. He went to the window, pulled back the curtains, looked out. He left then, and went downstairs.

When I did get up to go deliver my papers,

almost a half hour after Andrew'd left, it'd started raining again. I got my rain jacket out of the closet and went downstairs.

I went through the kitchen and got my canvas sack out of the utility closet. I tucked the sack under my arm and went out to the garage.

My bike wasn't there. I looked all over the garage, there wasn't a bike in it. Daddy made us keep it pretty neat, and there wasn't anything it could be parked behind. Anyway, I knew where I'd left it. Now that I'd waited so late to deliver my papers, my customers were probably wondering if I was going to show up at all.

I felt in my pockets to see if I had any money. I did. I slipped the hood of the rain jacket tighter on my head and went into the next block to the bus stop.

Because of the rain, it was very dark when I got home that night.

I went in. The storm door hissed shut behind me. I was soaked in spite of my rain jacket. I stood in the doorway, dripping wet.

Mama and Daddy and Andrew were in the living room. At first, nobody said a word. Then, Mama said to Andrew, "What?"

I stayed in the doorway. It was like they hadn't seen me, hadn't heard me come in. I looked at Mama and Daddy. Their faces were sad like there'd been an announcement of a death. Of a close relative.

"I couldn't help it, Mama," Andrew said. He put his hands in his pockets and paced the room. I got the feeling he'd been pacing like that a long time. You could almost see the path he'd cut in the carpet. "I'd just delivered a prescription, and I went back to the drugstore. I got another prescription. When I left, the bike was gone."

"What — what's the matter?" I asked. It was like I wasn't even there. My voice sounded funny, far away, even to me. "What?" I asked again.

None of them paid any attention to me. Whatever Andrew was talking about must've been real important. I stayed in the doorway and peeled off the rain jacket. I was getting cold since I was wet like that. I went to the stairs, climbed. I was halfway up, but Andrew's next words brought me down again. I stood in the doorway. My rain jacket was crumpled and dripping in my left hand.

Andrew was saying, "Alex's bike was gone. There was nobody on the street. I even looked down the alleyway. But I didn't see anyone."

I threw the rain jacket against the storm door. The outside of the door was already wet. My wet jacket made the inside wet. It fell in a crumple at the bottom of the door.

"You didn't lose my bike, Andrew?"

"Somebody stole it this afternoon. I — I called the police."

I thought of how many times I'd told him to

lock it, not to bother my bike at all. "What were you doing?"

"I already told Mama what I was doing."

I went over to my brother, stood directly in front of him. "You'll just have to get me another bike. It's bad enough I had to ride the bus to throw papers when I had a bike. But now, it's gone forever."

"Look," Andrew said, coming toward me. "I lost my job, but I'm getting another one. I'll help you get a new bike."

I grabbed the front of his shirt. "Listen to me. Don't you ever put your hands on anything that belongs to me. Ever again. Do you hear me? And I'm tired of you beating me up just to have things your own way. I got feelings, too." I started shaking him. That's when Mama grabbed me. She held me with one hand and pried my fingers from Andrew's shirt with her other hand. I was still able to give Andrew a push before I let him go. He slipped backwards, but didn't fall. Daddy caught him, held him.

I tried to edge up closer to Andrew, but Mama wouldn't let me go. She had her arms 'round my chest, gripping so hard like I was gonna fly away. All I could do was stare at Andrew. He blinked fast, twice, like he was gonna cry.

I twisted from side to side. "Mama, let me go. I'm all right." She let me go. I wheeled 'round, headed to the stairs. I turned my head but didn't

54

stop walking. "I'm going to have to give up my route. If I have to ride the bus every day, I won't be making any money."

I climbed the stairs slowly, as if they were made of eggshells and my weight would break them. I heard Andrew call me. I didn't turn around. I didn't stop until I was upstairs in my room. It was hot in the house, but I closed the bedroom door. Actually, I slammed the door. I slammed it so hard the house rocked. The goldfish bowl on my desk skittered to the edge. I lay back on my bed.

After a while, I don't know how long, I got up, filled the bathtub. I peeled off my damp clothes and climbed in. The bath felt good and I could stay in it until I woke up! Until I realized all this was a dream. Andrew hadn't really lost my bike at all. It was a nightmare. The bath would wake me, and I'd find my bike hadn't been stolen at all.

I was going to stay in the tub until Andrew went to bed. Till he went to sleep. Although I was getting a little waterlogged, I didn't move.

I could hear Mama and Daddy talking to Andrew, but I couldn't make out what was being said. Then, Andrew came upstairs, walking slowly, hardly making a sound on the stairs. It was like he was a burglar breaking in to get the silverware to go along with my bicycle.

Andrew jiggled the bathroom doorknob. I didn't move. I didn't say anything. He went away.

When I'd given him time to fall asleep, I got

out of the tub, toweled myself off, and went down-stairs.

Mama and Daddy were sitting on the sofa. The light was out and the room was kind of dark. I sat in the big chair by the table at the door. I reached up to turn on the ginger jar lamp, but thought I'd feel better without a lot of light. It wasn't really real dark in the room on acccount the door was still opened and the street lamp was throwing some light in. The street lamp was closest to Mrs. Pet-taway's house but it lit our living room well enough, I guess.

"Alex, are you all right?" Mama asked.

"I guess so."

"It was wrong what Andrew did. He's promised to help you save money to buy a new bike."

"Yeah, I bet he will," I said, and slumped farther down in the chair. My head was pressed against the back of the chair, my legs stretched out. "He never keeps his promise."

"I think he will this time," Daddy said. "In fact, I know he will if he ever wants to go to the lot again."

I didn't say anything. All I could do was hope that Andrew would keep his word. But I wasn't gonna count on it. Andrew acted like a stranger to me sometimes. I could hardly believe how we used to pal around together.

I still wasn't sleepy. Mostly, I didn't want to go up into the room with Andrew. Maybe he was asleep; I didn't know for sure. Mama and Daddy were talking to me, but I barely heard what they were saying.

After a while, I said, "I'd better go to bed. Sunday papers are harder to deliver than weekday papers." There were more customers for the Sunday paper. I stood up, stretched, and headed for the stairs.

I wondered if I should go on and try to keep my route. But I didn't say anything except, "Goodnight, Mama, Daddy."

I went up the stairs, feeling like my weight was suddenly twice what it used to be.

In the room, the light was on and I could hear Andrew snoring, not as loud as before, but loud enough. I got a football that was in the corner near his desk and threw it at him. He raised up, a goofy look on his face. "Turn over," I said.

He pushed the football to the floor and turned over. He went to sleep again, not snoring this time. I crossed the room, turned out the light, and went to bed.

Nine

The bath I'd taken earlier woke me up all right. I spent most of the night tossing and turning. But no matter which way I tossed or turned, I still didn't have a bicycle.

I lay in the dark room and listened to raindrops spatter the roof and heard the house settling. And thought of the days when I'd have to spend two-fifty to ride the bus to throw papers. Two dollars and a half every day is a lot of money. I couldn't quit or I'd never get a bicycle. Even if there's a miracle and Andrew helps me save money.

When I finally fell asleep, I must've been dreaming about how broke I was. It was the first thing to come into my mind when I woke up Sunday morning.

I looked over at Andrew. He'd turned on his

58

back again and was snoring a lot louder than before.

I swung my feet over the side of the bed and
got up. I had Sunday papers to deliver. Stacks and
stacks of them were on a corner 'cross town, already waiting for me. Probably. When I had my
bike, I'd had to make two trips. Stuff as many
papers into my canvas sack and hang it on the
buddy seat of my bike, then deliver them. Then
I'd go back to the drop point and do it all over
again.

I got dressed, brushed my teeth, and went
downstairs. I didn't feel like eating anything, so I
just left to get the papers out of the way.

It's a funny thing. When I got home that afternoon, Andrew was 'round back washing the car.
He was up to his elbows in a big bucket of soapy
water. His clothes were all wet where he'd sloshed
himself, trying to hurry and get through, I guess.
Anyway, his gang was over in the lot playing softball.

"Hi, Alex," he said. "You gonna help me?"

"No." I went inside and hung my canvas sack
on a hook in the kitchen utility closet.

I grabbed a banana out of the bowl on the table
and went out and stood on the back steps. By this
time, Andrew had finished washing the car and
was polishing it.

"Look, Andrew," I said. "You missed a spot."

"I'm missing a good softball game is what I'm doing," he said, but he did go over the spot he'd missed.

I stood on the steps, munching my banana, and watched Andrew polish the car. When he'd finished and it was sparkling in the sun, he came over to the steps and said, "Alex, I really will help you get a new bike — "

"How?" I interrupted him.

"I don't know how, but I will. You'll see."

We were quiet then. Andrew should've gone to the lot, but he didn't. He started putting away the rags and polish. He rolled up the garden hose, hung it in the garage. I rolled my banana peel into a ball and pitched it clear 'cross the yard into the garbage can.

"Wow!" Andrew said, and grinned. "Almost as good as me."

He was still smiling when he came back to the steps. "How come you and Thrash don't come to the lot with us anymore?"

"I been kind of busy. My paper route, school — "

"I wish you'd come," he said. He turned, went 'round the corner of the house, headed for the lot.

Ten

Of all the dumb luck, I thought, when I got up the next morning. Andrew was sleeping like a baby over on his bed. I hadn't slept hardly at all, because Andrew snored so loud. Every time I dozed off, I'd remember I didn't have a bicycle. And to make bad matters worse, on Sunday Mama hadn't had company, and there weren't any extra dishes for Andrew to wash.

I looked at my watch. I could've stayed in bed another hour, but I got up and got ready for school. Until I got a new bike, I'd always have to get up early to walk to school. I couldn't even ride to school with Thrash anymore. And after school, I'd always have to get the papers out of the way first and do my homework second. The only good thing about this mess I was in was that school was almost over. And I wouldn't have to do homework until September.

But summer is the time I needed a bike most. Last summer, me and Thrash used to ride down to the river to fish. Or just ride around. All that was gone now.

I finished dressing and went downstairs.

In the kitchen, I drank two glasses of orange juice. I didn't feel like eating. It was too hot. And it was only 7:30 in the morning.

Five minutes later, I left for school. I didn't go up and wake Andrew. He always needed someone to wake him. But I didn't. "Andrew," I said and stopped. I thought maybe we could walk a few blocks together, but I changed my mind 'cause we weren't going to be friends again. I grabbed my books and left for school.

The sun blazed down, burning into my neck as I walked the twelve blocks to school. Boy! Did I miss my bike.

I was gonna have to save all summer *and* winter now. A bicycle seemed as far out of reach as an English racing car. I still had a little money saved, but I couldn't buy any old bike. I wanted a good one. One better than the one Andrew'd lost. Maybe Mama and Daddy will make Andrew help me buy another bike. If Andrew only keeps his word. . . .

When I got home that afternoon, I went straight to the closet and got the plastic orange juice jar. It seemed lighter somehow. Maybe because my bike was gone, I was imagining all sorts of weird things.

I carried the jar to my desk, opened it. I counted the money. And I didn't have the amount I thought I had. I wasn't imagining anything. Just to be sure, I counted my money again. And again. Most of it was dollar bills and quarters. The roll of bills should've been thicker, the coins heavier. They weren't.

I was so absorbed in counting my money, I didn't hear Mama come in.

"What are you up to, Alex?"

"Just counting my money."

"It didn't sink in that your father and I said Andrew would help you, did it?"

"Mama — "

"Yes, he will," Mama said. "Or else. He's checking other stores, trying to find a part-time job."

"Andrew? Really?" I started stuffing the money back into the jar. I didn't know Andrew was actually looking for a job. I thought the drugstore job just kind of fell into his lap.

Mama said, "I'm certain he'll get one." She felt into the pocket of her house dress, pulled out a folded piece of paper. "Listen, the stores are open late tonight. Stop and pay on this layaway for me."

"Yes, ma'am." I took the check and the layaway receipt and put it into my wallet.

"It saves me a trip to town."

After Mama left, it hit me. Why didn't I put the

rest of my money on my bike? Put it on layaway?

I poured the money back out of the jar and smoothed the bills and put them into my wallet. I stuffed as many of the coins into my pockets as I could. While I was doing that, I happened to glance at the page out of the bike catalog that I'd stuck into the mirror. I snatched it down.

I folded the clipping, pushed it into my pocket. Then I started out. My pockets were fat and bulging, but I didn't care.

Later, after my papers were delivered, I went to the shopping center to pay on Mama's layaway. And pay on my bike.

In the bike department, there were rows and rows of bicycles — every kind I could imagine. The store was nearly empty and I browsed awhile.

"Young man, may I help you?" the clerk asked when he saw me gawking at all the bikes.

"Just looking," I said. He went back to arranging things on the counter. I checked the price tag on a gold bike with skinny wheels and frame. It was exactly like the one Thrash had shown me in my bike catalog, but the price was more. This bike costed $399.95; that was $49.95 more than in my bike catalog. I whistled softly and moved away.

I found the bike that was in my clipping. It was blue with a white stripe down each fender. And it was the exact same price as in my catalogue. I went to the clerk and told him what I wanted to do. He wrote my name, address, and phone number on a form he pulled off a stack by the cash register. I signed the form and counted out the money to him.

"My, my," he said, taking the money. "With regular payments, you'll be riding your new bike real soon. Real soon." He rang the money, deposited it into the cash register.

I grinned, took my receipt, folded it. When it was safe and sound in my wallet, I felt a thousand times better. Although my wallet was thin and empty without the money, I still felt good. After another look at my bike, I left the store.

I paid on Mama's layaway then went to the bus stop. I waited a good while, but my bus wouldn't come. Fifteen minutes later, I started walking home. I'd catch the bus at another stop.

I'd walked several blocks, stopping to look behind me to see if my bus was coming. That's when I saw Andrew. He and the guys were coming out of Rolf-Sinclair's theater — the one on Sixth and Henderson. Andrew was sharp in his light blue summer suit. The guys were dressed up, too. I'd left home long before Andrew and hadn't seen him since soon this morning.

Holding my one last newspaper — the one Mrs. Pettaway always bought — I ran and caught up with Andrew.

"Hey, Andrew! Man, let me have some money," I said, watching him take a bite out of a giant movie candy bar. "You got any more?"

"Naw, man, I ain't got no more." He laughed real slow like and started walking faster. I had to trot to keep up. I couldn't get him to look at me.

"Wasn't that a good movie?" I said, just making conversation. Andrew shrugged. He acted like he was in an awful big hurry. It was still light, and he'd have time to get in a game or two, if that's what was worrying him. I wondered where he'd gotten money from, anyway. We didn't get our allowances until Friday.

"Andrew, didn't you hear what I said?"

"Yeah. Yeah," he said, finally. "It was a good movie." He didn't slow down. If I didn't know better, I'd say he was trying to shake me off.

Mac waddled up beside me. I always get the feeling that he was wobbling instead of walking. He said, "That was the best sci-fi flick I seen since Godzilla ate up Tokyo." He fished 'round in the big tub of popcorn he'd brought out of the movies, popped kernels into his mouth.

"Your appetite's sorta like Godzilla's," Mungo said. He grinned and pushed the end of his necktie into his pants so it wouldn't flap out when he walked. He slowed down and fell into step with me. I certainly wasn't keeping up with Andrew. Anyway, I didn't think Mungo was gonna try something with Andrew around. But you never knew with Mungo.

I knew Mungo wasn't thinking about me when

he reached out, snatched Mac's tub of popcorn. "Gimme some of that."

"Hey!" Mac yelled. He snatched the tub back so fast that yellowish-white kernels spilled out, rolling on the sidewalk.

Mungo threw a fistful of popcorn into his mouth. We were now walking side by side, me and Mungo. "I ain't forgot how you did me with those sentences. That old lady Reid added a thousand more to them. And I gotta go to summer school since you didn't write my essay."

"You oughta get your homework," Sammy Minor told him.

Mungo grabbed Sammy in the collar, drawing Sammy's face clear up to his. Their noses were touching.

"I was just playing," Sammy said. "Just playing. You know me, Mungo."

Mungo let go of Sammy. Sammy was trying to unwrinkle his shirt front.

To me, Mungo said, "Well, I ain't playing with you. I'm gonna get you. When you least expect it. When it's nobody but you and me." He pointed a bony brown finger in my face and stuck out his lip to show he meant business.

Although I was tired, I started walking faster, trying to catch up with Andrew. I wasn't scared of skinny old Mungo, but no matter what, I wasn't about to do any work for him. I just wanted to get home, lie down, cool off.

We'd walked so long, so many blocks, that we were almost home. I guessed my bus must've passed me up somewhere.

At the entrance to our dead-end street, we split up. Andrew ran on ahead so he could change his clothes.

"Meet me in the lot," Andrew shouted after his friends. He'd taken off his necktie and coat and was starting to unbutton his shirt. He knew to change his clothes before going out to play. Mama would've killed him if he got his suit dirty.

When I got to the stoop, I took careful aim and flung Mrs. Pettaway's paper onto her porch. It made all kinds of racket when it thumped against her screen door. But she didn't holler for me to come read it to her. Anyway, I didn't feel like reading to her and having Andrew tease me about it.

I opened the storm door and threw my canvas sack on the floor by the lamp table. Mama was gonna have a fit, but I didn't care. I was too tired, I had to sit down and rest.

I must've rested about fifteen minutes, but I was still tired. I could barely climb the stairs to my room. I met Andrew halfway up. He was pulling on a T-shirt and moving like a tornado.

He jabbed me in the side when he passed me.

"Quit, boy. It's too hot. And I'm too tired."

He went on outdoors without looking back. I was in my room taking off my gym shoes when I heard the storm door hiss shut.

Eleven

I got off the bed and crossed to the window. I pulled the curtains aside and propped them on top of my desk with books. I raised the window as high as it'd go. There wasn't much air coming in, but it was better than nothing. I went back to the bed and lay down. I was about to doze off when Mama came into the room.

I sat up and slipped the layaway receipt out of my wallet and gave it to her. I said, "I put my bike on layaway."

She smiled and said, "Good, good." Then, she looked 'round the room a bit. And I knew what was coming. She wanted the room clean. But I was wrong, she didn't mention the room. She said, "Alex, I'm concerned about you staying indoors so much. In fact, too much."

"I know I should go out, Mama, but—"

"No buts about it." She walked 'round the room

69

like it was her first visit. "I don't know what I'm going to do about you boys and this room. It looks like a cyclone hit it. I just ironed Andrew's shirts. What're they doing on the floor?" She picked two shirts off the floor. "Where's that Andrew? Never mind. He's where he always is. He knows he needs permission to go to the lot."

She went to the window, tried to push it higher. She stuck her head out the window and yelled, "Andrew! Get up here! Don't let me have to come down there."

Almost before she'd pulled her head back into the room, I heard Andrew running up the stairs. He made the old stairs creak like they were gonna break.

"Don't you come in here like that."

"All right, Mama," Andrew said.

"Clean up this room. I'll be in the bathroom giving Bonnie a bath. When I get through, I want this room clean. This floor better be clean enough to eat off."

"Yes, ma'am," Andrew and I said at the same time.

Mama went out. I could hear her filling the bathtub. Andrew stayed in the doorway, his hands on the door jambs.

Finally, he crossed to his side of the room and stretched out on his bed.

Mama's house shoes flip-flopped down the hall-way, coming toward our room. Andrew popped off his bed so fast, he was like a piece of bread shooting out of a toaster gone haywire.

"Umph! I see you boys haven't got started." Mama stood in the doorway, her hands on her hips. She shook her head. "Alex, go get Bonnie some milk. Get a half gallon. Hurry before the store closes." She handed me a five-dollar bill.

When I got back and set the milk in the refrigerator, I guiltily stuffed the last of my ice-cream cone into my mouth. I had seventy-five cents left from the last time I rode the bus to throw papers. I used it to buy an ice-cream cone. I'd promised to save every spare penny. I went upstairs, hoping Andrew'd started cleaning.

He hadn't. He was still on his bed. The room looked messier than it had before I left.

"Didn't you even start?"

"Naw. I had to wait for you." He was lying on his back, his hands under his head. His feet were crossed at the ankles. He wiggled them from side to side. He didn't get up.

I stood in the doorway, throwing a quarter up and catching it. Each time, I'd throw it higher than before. I was pretty good at catching it.

"How much money Mama gave you to get that milk?"

"Five dollars," I said.

"Give me that quarter. That's mine."

"How you figure?" I asked him, and went on throwing the quarter up and catching it. Andrew got off the bed real slow. He came over to me.

"You catch a quarter real good," he said. "Real good." Then he caught Mama's quarter, midair.

"I'll give it back as soon as you clean this room." He started downstairs soft so Mama wouldn't hear him. Suddenly, he stopped. A step creaked. "My half, too." He made a fist at me. "Or else." He flipped the quarter in the air, a lot higher than I'd done. He wasn't good at catching it. It rolled over into a corner. He bent and picked it up. He'd tossed it into the air a third time, when Mama came out of the bathroom. She had Bonnie wrapped in a towel in one arm. With the other hand, she started to close the bathroom door, but what she did was catch the quarter before it got halfway to Andrew's hand again.

"Now, if you and Alex are through playing with my money, I'll take my change." I gave her three dollars and ninety-one cents. "I'll be in Bonnie's room dressing her while you're cleaning."

Andrew picked up an armload of magazines and took them downstairs. It was taking him so long to come back, I went to the window and looked out. Sure enough, there was Andrew, crossing the street to the vacant lot. He must've gone out through the kitchen door so Mama wouldn't hear the storm door hiss shut.

I looked 'round the messy room and sat on one side of my bed. There wasn't anything I could do now. Except clean.

Twelve

But I couldn't clean the room. No sirree. I didn't live in it alone. I didn't mess it up by myself. I hadn't messed it up at all. I sure wasn't gonna clean Andrew's half, too. No matter what.

I gave my part of the room the once over again just to make sure. I always made my bed as early as possible. Andrew's bed looked like it'd never been made. It was lumpy and the pillow was at the foot. The only time Andrew helped me work was in the yard. And I wasn't gonna let him walk on me again. 'Cause when I got my new bike, he'd do the same as he did when I had my old one.

I went to the window, stared out. I started to yell down for Andrew the way Mama'd done, but I went downstairs, stood on the stoop.

"Andrew!" I yelled as loud as I could.

He stopped playing ball, looked over at me. I raised my hand, becked for him. He said something to the guys that I couldn't hear. Then, in that bouncing way he had of walking, he came across the street. The guys went on playing ball.

"You got to help clean," I said.

He wrinkled his forehead, stuck out his lip. He yanked open the storm door so hard, it banged against the Wandering Jew in the big stone pot on the corner of the stoop. He went upstairs. He walked slowly as if by some miracle, the room'd be cleaned by the time he got upstairs.

"Did Mama send you to get me?'

"No. I think she told you to help me clean."

"And I won't tell you again," Mama said from Bonnie's room. "Dirty clothes goes into the hamper. Clean clothes goes in the closet on hangers or into drawers. I'll be in the backyard while Bonnie's taking a nap." She went downstairs.

After she'd left, I mentioned offhand that it was my money he'd used to go to the movies. No wonder he acted strange, I thought.

"No, it wasn't," Andrew said, starting to pick up his clothes and things.

"Where you get money?"

"I — borrowed it."

"From who?"

"It's none of your business."

"Then I'll go on thinking you took my money."

"If you had it lying 'round the house, I would've

74

taken it. But I don't know where you kept it."

"It *was* my money," I said. I went to the closet, got the almost empty bottle. A few pennies and dimes covered the bottom of the jar. "Look here. It was full of money, almost. Five-and ten-dollar bills, ones — mostly ones. Well, I put a brand-new bike on layaway."

My arm was shaking, rattling loose change in the jar. "Admit you took it, Andrew."

"No. 'Cause I didn't take much of it."

"Much of it? How much did you take?"

"Twenty dollars. Maybe twenty-five dollars." He stood up from where he'd been picking things off the floor. He said quickly, "I'm gonna pay it back. Every penny. I've got some money coming."

I got tired of holding the jar. I let it fall to the floor. It landed with a *thunk* right in front of him.

"Look, Alex, let's just clean this room. I've got something to do. And it has to be done today."

He set about busily to finish cleaning the room. It didn't seem to matter to him that I wasn't doing any work at all. I'd gone to my bed, lay down, my hands behind my head. I was thinking about the twenty-five dollars. If Andrew'd just pay it back, like he say, I could go get my bike.

He finally finished cleaning and grabbed clean clothes out of his dresser drawers, a pair of cut-off jeans, blue T-shirt, clean underwear. He went into the bathroom.

I must've dozed off, 'cause when I got up, Andrew was gone. It was still just barely light and the guys were playing by streetlight in the vacant lot. From the window, I looked at the guys carefully, but as far as I could tell, Andrew wasn't there. I didn't hear his mouth, either.

He didn't come back until late. We were in the living room. Bonnie played with her dolls on the floor. Mama couldn't sit still. Andrew'd never been away from home so late before. Mama kept going to the window, looking out. I could tell Daddy was worried, too, but he kept telling Mama to sit still.

"Adela," Daddy said, "You're making me nervous." But Mama still went to the window every now and then.

I kept glancing at my watch, but nothing any of us did made Andrew come home any sooner.

Along about a quarter to eleven, he came in. He was a sight to see. There was a bruise on the left side of his forehead. His right eye was red as a beet — the part that should've been white.

"Where've you been? What happened to your eye? You shouldn't be out so late," Mama said, trying to ask him everything at once.

He didn't answer any of her questions. He bounded up the stairs, three at a time. I followed, trying to get to him, see what'd happened.

Upstairs, he went into the bathroom. He looked into the mirror. He began to splash cold water on his face. He cupped his palm, filled it with water, held it to his eye.

By this time, Mama and Daddy were upstairs. We all crowded into the tiny bathroom.

"Son, what happened?" Daddy's voice sounded so sad, I would've thought he'd gotten hit in the eye himself.

When Andrew did say something, it wasn't about his eye. "I wouldn't've taken your money, but it was so hot. It was ninety-eight degrees. And humid. And Mungo and Mac and Sammy came 'round with their money and all dressed up. I had to go to the movies with them. They got air-conditioning down there. It was so cold in the theater, I could see my breath. It felt good, too. I couldn't talk about it when you met us. I just wanted to figure out a way to put your money back before you missed it. I couldn't, 'cause without your bicycle, I was just as lost as you was."

Mama stood in the doorway, wringing her hands. "But what happened to your eye?"

"I worked for two weeks at the drugstore on Elmwood. I was being paid good money. Without a bicycle, I couldn't deliver prescriptions anymore. The druggist also had me working as a stock boy. When I stopped by the other day to see if I could keep on as a stock boy, he'd hired a big sixteen-year-old boy with a driver's license. The only thing to do was to try to get your bike back. I was gonna buy my own bike. And I was gonna explain exactly why I needed your bike. Even pay your bus fare with my tips. The tips were really something. Folks give you two and three dollars just for bringing their medicines."

I thought about Mrs. Kirkland and the ten-dollar check. I knew how Andrew felt.

He turned to face me, the lobster-red eye was almost closed up. A tear slipped down his cheek. He wasn't crying, his eye was watering so bad. "I went to the drugstore, just looking 'round. That's where your bike was stolen. I stopped this boy who I thought I saw riding your bike. We started fighting. Then, his whole gang jumped me. It looked like guys were jumping out of the walls, coming at me."

"Andrew — " I didn't finish. I kept looking at his eye.

"I realized how mean I'd been to you lately. I took your bike without even asking you," Andrew said. "When I got the job, and he asked me if I had a bike, I told him I did. I guess I must've been a little jealous. You always stick to everything you set out to do. How many times I've had a paper route and didn't keep it?" He smiled then, but tears were coming out of his sore eye so bad, he turned his head and wiped at his eye with the back of his hand. He turned back 'round but his eye was still watering. I wanted to tell him it was all right, but I stood rooted to the spot like I'd suddenly started growing there. Andrew put a hand on my arm; I didn't shake it off. I didn't move. He went on, "If it'd been just that one boy, I could've beat him, made him give me your bike. Not for me, but for you. I know he was the one who took it." He sniffled and snatched a tissue out of the box on the bathroom vanity, blew his nose.

Finally, I did move. I put my hands on his shoulders. Whatever I said or did wouldn't seem to help. Wouldn't get rid of how hurt he looked. How mad he seemed.

"I never meant for anybody to steal my brother's bike. Even when they were beating me up, I couldn't think about anything except getting your bike back. I hoped for a miracle. But they just kept on beating me to a pulp until the police came."

"The police brought you home?" Mama asked.

"Yes. They wanted to take me to the hospital, but I said I wanted to come home. I asked the police not to come in. They said okay, this time. I was kind of scared you would've thought I was halfway dead if you got a call from the hospital. I know how nervous you get sometimes."

Mama tried to smile, but it didn't quite come off. She grabbed tissues out of the box and gently dabbed Andrew's eye.

Seeing his eye red and swollen like that made me want to cry myself, but I didn't. I could feel my eyes getting full.

We were quiet, then.

Daddy broke the silence by saying, "Come on, I'm taking you to the emergency room." He took Andrew by the arm and they started out.

Andrew held his palm cupped over his eye so as not to damage it more. He looked back at me, then went on downstairs with Daddy.

After he and Daddy left, I took a bath and went to bed. But there was no sleep for me that night. I lay still in the bed thinking that Andrew had gotten hurt pretty bad trying to get my bike back. He didn't even have to do it at all. It meant that Andrew still liked me. At least, a little.

I lay on my back in the almost dark room. There was a little bit of light from the streetlight in front of Mrs. Pettaway's house. I couldn't get comfortable until I heard the sound of Daddy's old Chevy.

Thirteen

The next day after I'd delivered my papers and tried to do my homework, I went over to Mrs. Pettaway's. I gave her the one last newspaper.

She was already sitting on her porch in the shade, rocking slowly in the glider. She unfolded the paper from its tomahawk shape and tried to fan with it.

After a while, she said, "You feel like reading to me, Alex?"

"Yes, ma'am," I told her, but not feeling like doing anything at all.

I opened out the paper. It was still pretty well-creased, and I rubbed it across my thigh, trying to smooth it out some.

"Read the headlines."

I read them. To my ears, my voice sounded

funny, like my heart wasn't in reading.

After I fidgeted with the paper some more, Mrs. Pettaway grabbed it away from me. She folded it in half, held it on her lap. "Boy, what's wrong with you? Your face was as long as my arm when you first stepped up on my porch. If you blink those great big eyes, you gonna flood my yard."

I looked at Mrs. Pettaway. She sat on the edge of the glider, grinning, knowing.

To tell the truth, I didn't know where to start. I sniffled and opened my mouth. I closed it again, words whirling 'round, tumbling together in my head. I didn't know whether to start with my bike or with Andrew. I dived in.

"Andrew been so weird lately. I thought he took my bike just being mean, but it turns out, he got a job delivering prescriptions. For a drugstore."

"I've seen him riding 'round on your bike," Mrs. Pettaway said.

"He still spends a lot of time at the lot. I didn't know he was working. He should've told me what he was doing. We could've decided something together."

"That would've been good. But you see, Andrew real independent. Maybe he thinks you lean on him too much. I 'member when you and your family first moved here. Wherever you and Andrew went you were holding hands. You were little boys then, and it was good to see a big brother see after his little brother. Like you do with Bonnie now." She fanned with the newspaper.

"Andrew'll soon be interested in girls," she said. "And you won't be at the same time he is."

I sat there, listening, my mouth hung open. "Andrew?" I said.

Mrs. Pettaway nodded.

"Now, you take delivering prescriptions. You see, I think that starts him on the road to a more independent type of work. He wants to be in charge sometimes."

"He's just a little boy. He can't be too independent."

"You see that, Alex. You still thinking of him as a little boy. How do you see yourself?"

I grinned.

"You come over and read the paper to me. You can go all over the city by yourself, if you had to. Could you do that five years ago?"

I didn't say anything. I tried to think of going across town five years ago. I couldn't do it. I would've been too scared. Scared of getting lost, I guess.

"People always change. They don't stand still any more than times does." She shifted in the rickety old glider, put the paper on the seat beside her.

"I see him out there playing ball with boys bigger than he is. He gives them orders. He just wants to take charge sometimes. And you resist. I bet you a lot like him."

I smiled at that. "Mrs. Pettaway, I think it wasn't right that he should go playing cops and robbers. I'd already accepted that my bike was stolen."

"Yes. And a lot of things get stolen. I suppose the police'll look around for it."

"Yes, ma'am, but a lot of things don't ever turn up again. And I don't want to have to give up my route. I like it very much."

"I know you do. I know you do," Mrs. Pettaway said and nodded at the same time.

"I guess it won't hurt me to deliver papers on the bus for a while. If I don't spend my money for all kinds of things I don't really need, I'll be able to save for a new bicycle."

"Our difficulties help us to build character," Mrs. Pettaway said.

I stood up, stretched. "It's getting late," I said. "Good-night, Mrs. Pettaway."

I went home and went upstairs and tackled the mountain of homework before me. Only I couldn't concentrate on homework. I was still mad with Andrew, still upset about my bicycle. What I really wanted to do was beat up Andrew. Maybe I'd feel better, and could do my homework. I closed the book and leaned back in my chair. It was gonna be a long night. A very long night.

Fourteen

I was surprised that Andrew'd gone to school. I don't think I would've, even if Andrew did say I was in love with school. I didn't know he'd gone until he caught up with me when I was walking home that afternoon.

I was about to turn onto our dead-end street, when I heard someone running. I turned, and it was Andrew.

"Hey, Alex, you can walk pretty fast."

He fell into step beside me. "I thought you were at home in bed."

"Naw. I thought I'd go on and make these last few days."

"You going to lie down now, huh?"

"I guess so."

When we got home, he stayed on the stoop,

looking out at the lot. The guys were already there. They must've left school and gone directly to the lot.

Andrew went on inside, dropped his books on the coffee table, then went upstairs.

Mama passed him on the stairs, dressed to go out. "Watch Bonnie, Andrew. I'm going to the market," she said.

While I was getting my canvas sack out of the kitchen utility closet, Andrew came downstairs carrying Bonnie. He followed Mama outside. I rolled up my bag, tucked it under my arm. I checked to see if I had enough money for bus fare.

"Hey, Alex," Andrew yelled. "Come on. You got a ride."

I ran outside. Mama usually didn't have the car. She must've driven Daddy to school. Sometimes she did that, but not very often.

Since Mama was driving me to pick up my papers, I knew I'd get them delivered in record time. And I did. It was barely six o'clock when I got home from the bus stop.

I didn't think Andrew'd play ball with one eye, but he did. Just as I was about to go into the house, I saw Bonnie first. She was sitting on a patch of grass, playing with her teddy bear. She sat quietly, her back to me. Her bright yellow playsuit gleamed so much in the bright sun, it almost blinded me. I stood on the stoop, watching.

Bonnie threw the teddy bear aside and crawled

deeper into the grass. The grass wasn't all that tall, but you never knew what could happen to someone as little as Bonnie. She sat in a clump of grass, picking buttercups.

I watched her for a good little while. That's when the idea hit me.

While Andrew and the guys were still at the opposite end of the lot, I snuck across the street and took Bonnie up. I put a finger across my lips and said, "Shhh." She liked that and I knew she'd be quiet.

As I headed 'cross the street with Bonnie, I stole a glance at the team. They hadn't even noticed me. I went on across the street and took Bonnie upstairs. I put her into her crib, tied a bib 'round her neck and gave her a chocolate Popsicle, her favorite.

I went out to the stoop and yelled, "Andrew! Where's Bonnie?"

Right then, Andrew stopped playing and looked through the grass.

From where I stood, I could see him frantically searching in the grass. I've never seen Andrew act so scared before. He ran over to me, grabbed the front of my shirt.

"Alex, she was right there on the grass, playing." He pointed to the lot. "You gotta help me find her." He peeped behind me and looked into the living room, then back to the lot. "Help me look." I thought he was gonna cry. But he let go of my shirt and started running 'round like a dog chasing its tail.

I stayed in the doorway, my lip tucked between my teeth so I wouldn't laugh. I almost did it anyway and bit down on my lip harder.

Finally when it felt like I was gonna burst if I didn't laugh out loud, I really let loose.

"What did you do with her?" he asked in his angriest voice.

"Nothing. I haven't seen her since she was on the grass."

"A brother won't stand 'round acting like you doing if his sister really gone." Andrew pushed past me and ran into the kitchen. He stopped short when he saw that Mama and Daddy were back. "Hi," he said to them.

He raced out of the kitchen like his feet were greased. He went upstairs, three at a time. I heard him push open the door to Bonnie's room so fast, he banged it against the wall. The whole house trembled on its foundations.

"What's the matter with that boy?" Daddy asked nobody in particular.

I didn't say anything. From the top of the stairs, Andrew yelled, "Alex! Come here, Alex!" I didn't move. He came downstairs again.

Leaning close to me, he whispered, "Old loggy-headed boy, I'm gonna get you for that. If it's the last thing I do." He made a fist, shook it at me. He pushed his fist against my nose. "I'm gonna hit you in them big eyes. I got just one eye right now, but I'm gonna close both of yours for you."

I started laughing again. I laughed so hard, I had to hold my sides. But Andrew didn't laugh. I thought I was playing a good trick on him, getting even for some of the mean and nasty things he did to me. But he wouldn't laugh. I started feeling a little silly. I wiped my smile away. I was glad he hadn't punched me. He could've, but I knew he wouldn't with Mama and Daddy there to referee. Anyhow, I was in no mood for fighting. To tell the truth, what I'd done seemed like a very Andrew kind of thing to do. But he was really concerned about Bonnie, I guess. I hope. I'm sure of it.

I still felt bad about that little trick, but the excitement wasn't over for the day yet. After supper, Mama and Daddy went 'round the corner to a neighbor's. I had to wash dishes, therefore Bonnie was left with me 'cause as soon as Andrew'd checked the kitchen calendar to make sure it wasn't his turn to wash dishes, he did ninety running over to the lot. One day, I thought, he was gonna go over there and nobody'd show up to play ball with him.

When the house was empty except for Bonnie and me, I put her in the living room in her playpen so I could keep an eye on her while I cleaned the kitchen.

I scraped the dishes and put them into the sink. I squirted in a few drops of dishwashing liquid, and turned on the tap. Soon, the scent of lemon filled the air as the water got all bubbly.

When the sink was almost full, I turned off the tap, grabbed the sponge and started washing. I gazed out the window over the sink every now and then for something to take my mind off the job. Dishwashing is the most boring job ever invented.

Halfway through the dishes, something like a cloud caught my eye: over to the right — Mrs. Pettaway's house. I leaned over the sink and peeped 'round. I could see Mrs. Pettaway's porch good cause her house jutted back farther than ours.

Big puffs of smoke were shooting off Mrs. Pettaway's porch. I didn't bother to dry my hands. I threw the sponge down. I called the fire department. I grabbed Bonnie out of her playpen. She was kinda heavy, but if Mrs. Pettaway was in any kinda danger, I couldn't take Bonnie with me. Or leave her alone.

Closing the door behind me, I dashed across to the lot and put Bonnie in Andrew's arms. I did it so fast, he didn't have time to say a word. I raced back 'cross to Mrs. Pettaway's house. I didn't even know if she was at home or not.

Once I got up on her porch, and my heart stopped pounding so loud, I could hear her radio. She was in there all right. I made a fist and banged on her door.

No answer. I banged again. And again. Her radio went off.

"I'm coming. I'm coming," she said, real loud.

She seemed to think everybody is hard of hearing 'cause she is, I guess.

"Alex, what's the matter? Did I send you to the store?" she asked, when she'd opened the door.

"No, ma'am," I said. "I think your back porch is on fire."

"Wha—what?" She turned and headed through to the back of her house.

"Come on, Mrs. Pettaway. I've already called the fire department." But she still had her head set on going to see for herself. "No. No, ma'am." I was shouting now. "Come with me." I grabbed her arm and half-dragged her out on the front porch.

By now, the fire trucks were flying along the street, sirens screaming. I led Mrs. Pettaway next door to my house. Andrew was sitting on the stoop, holding Bonnie. Mac, Mungo, and Sammy were sitting on the bottom steps. The football lay on the grass, forgotten.

Seated on the sofa in the living room next to Mrs. Pettaway, I could see she was still scared. She kept her hands busy folding and unfolding the corner of her starched white apron that she always wore, even to the store.

I guess she was pretty lonesome in that great big house with Mr. Pettaway dead almost thirty years. I think that's why she wanted me to read to her — just for company.

I left her inside with Bonnie and went through the back and looked over toward her house. The firemen were still poking 'round in the piles of old magazines and newspapers, making sure the fire was out.

People from all over the neighborhood were standing 'round watching. They'd been that way since the first scream of the sirens. A policeman kept telling them: "Stay back! Not too close!" but they kept pushing forward.

It wasn't a real bad fire, just the magazines and newspapers Mrs. Pettaway'd read through the years and couldn't bear to part with. Now, they were nothing but so much burnt trash. Good thing the papers were damp from being outside. They mostly just smoked instead of burning completely up.

The fire chief later told her to throw them away. As if it was the least little thing. Mrs. Pettaway must've kept them to look over them, remembering what she'd read or had read to her. She had a stack that came up to my waist. That must've been about two-three years worth of papers.

When the crowd saw that Mrs. Pettaway's whole house wasn't going to go up in flames, they took off in different directions. You could hear doors opening and closing all over the neighborhood.

I turned and looked at Mrs. Pettaway. She'd come to look at the fire, too, but she stood in the kitchen doorway of my house. You could still smell wet, burnt paper in the air. A breeze came up and stirred Mrs. Pettaway's hair. Maybe it was a breeze. Maybe she was still scared.

"Mrs. Pettaway, why don't you spend the night with us?" I asked, searching my mind for a place for her to sleep. I couldn't let her go back to her house. She must've been scared to death. "Come on. We got plenty of room. I'll walk over with you to get your things."

While I was in her living room, I heard her shuffling 'round upstairs. Then, a few minutes later, she came down with a battered brown suitcase. Stickers of the places she'd been were plastered all over it, like Band-Aids. One sticker said, ROME. When I looked at it closer, I saw it said, ROME, GEORGIA. She must've traveled a lot when she was younger. Or when Mr. Pettaway was alive.

We left then. She locked the door, jiggled the knob to make sure. I took the suitcase out of her hand and walked on ahead of her, 'cross the lawn separating her yard from ours. The bag wasn't heavy.

Bonnie, Mrs. Pettaway, and I were in the living room again. I turned on the TV. "Do you want some pop?" I said.

"That I do," Mrs. Pettaway said, nodding slowly.

I got her a can of pop. Handing it to her, I said, "All we've got is Dr Pepper."

Her hands were shaking so, I had to pour some of the pop into the glass for her. I was careful to serve it on a tray with a napkin like Mama would've.

Mama and Daddy came home just as it was starting to get dark. It got dark sudden, like we were gonna have a lot of rain. We sure did need it. Maybe it'd be cooler at night.

"I heard sirens," Mama said. Then she saw Mrs. Pettaway. "Hello, Mrs. Pettaway."

Mrs. Pettaway nodded slowly.

I jumped up. "Mama, there was a small fire at Mrs. Pettaway's. I asked her to stay over."

"Good, son," Mama said.

Daddy smiled and asked Mrs. Pettaway if she had all the things she needed from her house.

"Yes. Alex was sweet enough to help me bring over a bag."

Daddy nodded.

Along about then, it started raining. Just a light mist. I could see it on the living room window. But, by the time sleeping arrangements were made, it was pouring. The rain didn't do anything about the heat. It seemed like it made things steam up more.

When we'd gone to bed, Andrew sweated so, he had to keep changing the bandage on his eye. It kept coming unglued. It got so bad, he just took it off and kept his eye closed.

It'd been such a night of excitement, I'd forgotten about being mad at Andrew. But then, I wasn't that much mad at him anymore. He did try to get my bike back. I turned over on my left side and went to sleep.

Fifteen

The last day of school had finally rolled 'round. Andrew thought it was such a swell day, he got up early. Even earlier than Daddy, and Daddy had students.

I heard Andrew stirring about in our room. Only stirring isn't the word. He kept dropping things, making all kinds of racket. That's what woke me.

"Quit some of that noise," I said. "I'm still trying to sleep." He didn't answer, but went right on clomping 'round the room. "What's the matter with you? A whole roomful of boys could dress quieter than you doing."

"Get up!" he commanded.

"I don't want to get up." I looked at my watch. "I can stay in bed twenty minutes longer."

"No, you can't."

He pulled open drawers, searched through them, and shut them again, not caring that clothes were hanging out every which way.

"Alex, get up." It wasn't a command. It sounded more like begging.

I raised up on an elbow, looked at him. He was dressed in a white sports shirt and white shorts. He'd just polished his white gym shoes. White shoe polish was on his hands and legs.

"I gotta have a note or else I won't get my report card."

"Tell Mama. Don't tell me."

"I can't tell Mama. How's it gonna look when I come home without a card?" He went to the dresser, checked his hair. "Besides, Mama don't know I didn't go to school that day. And I don't want her to know. She'll get mad and scream and yell and make me stay away from the lot." He looked at me for a long, long time, then said, "I'm already in enough trouble as it is."

"Huh?" I said.

"I didn't go to school that day 'cause I hadda go swimming with Mungo and Sammy."

"Maybe one of them'll write you a note."

He gave me a look that said I ought to shut my mouth. He sat on his bed, then jumped up again. He started making his bed. Without being told. It's gonna rain cats and dogs for sure when Andrew do some work. I cocked my head toward the window, listening. It wasn't raining now. I turned to look at Andrew. He was just about finished with his bed. When he was done, he picked up a pile of clothes he'd left scattered about the room. "What you gonna do?" I asked.

"When Mama and Daddy go downstairs, you gonna write me a note."

I lay back down. "No. Never." I meant it, too.

We were silent until we heard Mama and Daddy get up. "Boys! Get Up!" Daddy said as he went downstairs.

"We're up," I said.

Andrew went into their room and came back with typing paper and Daddy's fountain pen.

"Don't bother twisting my arm, 'cause I still won't write your note. 'Member how you changed your report card that time? You can write your own note." I got up.

He sat to his desk, unscrewed the cap on Daddy's fountain pen. He was practicing writing with the fountain pen. He would scribble a few sentences on a sheet of paper, read it over, then throw it in the waste basket.

By this time, I was dressed, except for socks and shoes. He'd started writing again, but he didn't ball this note up. I stood behind Andrew, reading the note over his shoulder. He wrote extra big like he thought a parent would've. This is what he wrote:

Dear Mrs. Cooke:
Andrew Walker couldn't report for school on May

*7th because I took him to the ophthalmologist.
Thank goodness he doesn't have to wear glasses.
Thank you.*

*Sincerely yours,
Adela M. Walker.*

It was perfect, except I thought the really large handwriting made it look like a child had written the note. He'd made me look up ophthalmologist.

He folded the note, stuck it into his shorts pocket. He took Daddy's fountain pen back to Daddy's desk.

When we returned home on that last day of school, it was ten-thirty. Andrew's letter must've worked. He held up his report card as if it was a hundred-dollar bill he'd found on the sidewalk.

"Isn't it good that school is out, little brother?" Andrew said when we'd gone upstairs. He grinned from ear to ear, teeth flashed.

Mama came upstairs with a load of clothes to iron. She was still on the stair when Andrew added, "No more getting out of bed before the sun is up — "

"Oh, yes, you will, too," Mama said. "This isn't a resort hotel." She set the basket of clothing on the landing, took the report cards we handed her. "These are great report cards. I'm proud of both of you. Now, clean your room before you go anywhere else."

About an hour later, when we were downstairs

98

again, Mama said, "Is the room clean?"

"Yes, ma'am," Andrew and I said.

Andrew moved toward the door, turned, and looked at me. "Are you coming to the lot? You ain't got homework and your papers don't go out till later."

"Maybe after a while."

I went upstairs to read some comic books I'd already read a hundred times. The storm door hissed shut as Andrew went out.

I was halfway through another space saga when I heard the storm door open again. It was Andrew. He came upstairs slow, like he was tired. I was lying on my bed. Andrew'd come upstairs almost to the top. He stood looking through the railings like a prisoner gazing through the bars of his cell.

He stared at me for a long, long time. I stared back. I wanted to ask him if he could play ball all right with one eye, but I didn't.

"Can you come over to the lot?" he asked.

"What's the matter?"

"Nothing. I just — thought you would."

We didn't say anything for a while. Andrew gazed through the railings. With my comic book flat on my chest, held in one hand, I started rolling the pages back, creasing them. Then Andrew said, "See you."

I finished reading the comic book and then left to get my newspapers delivered for another day.

Sixteen

I can't say that Andrew and I turned out to be the best of friends. I can't say we didn't have any more fights, 'cause we had a real set-to on the last Saturday in July. I'll never forget that day, 'cause I almost didn't get my bicycle.

I could only get my bicycle 'cause Andrew kept his word. He finally went a couple of weeks ago to pick up his pay from the drugstore, and he'd given me money. I paid it on my bike. If he hadn't given me money, I'd still been struggling trying to get my bike paid for.

My bike was the only thing on my mind that Saturday morning, and I don't see why we started fighting. Even Andrew'd been in a good mood. He didn't exactly have a new job, but he'd been helping out at the neighborhood grocery store. It was doing the same thing he'd done at the drugstore, so I guess he liked it all right. Mr. Mullins, the owner, usually called him in, but he hadn't called this Saturday, and I think Andrew was glad about that 'cause he had something else he wanted to do. He'd even got up hours before I did.

Around quarter to nine, I got up, dressed. Andrew was at the dresser looking into the mirror on account he had a new baseball cap. It was royal blue with a big white "W" on the front. "You got to keep Bonnie. I got a practice game."

"I told you last night I was going to get my bike first thing," I told Andrew.

"But this game is a chance of a lifetime," he said. "All the guys made the team. You will, too. I'm the captain. You can put your bike off till next week."

"I wanna get my bike."

"The store that's sponsoring us even got us these uniforms." Andrew took off the baseball cap, adjusted it, and put it back on. He had the jersey and pants and a baseball jacket draped 'cross his unmade bed. "How long can Mama be shopping, anyway?"

"I can't wait all weekend knowing I could have my bike today," I said.

"Just two more days. That ain't so long."

"To me it is."

"Didn't I give you money to help you?" Andrew asked.

"Yeah, but I want it today." I started to say, "If it wasn't for you, I wouldn't be in this mess." But what I said was, "I won't have to ride the bus this weekend. If I don't get my bike today, I'd have to spend five dollars of the money for bus fares. Besides, it takes the bus too long to come on Sundays."

I waited. He looked over at his baseball uniform on the bed. It looked out of place on such a lumpy bed.

"An hour, that's as long as it'll take me," I said. I thought of something Mama sometimes said when she sent us on errands for her: "I don't want to miss the time you're gone." I smiled at Andrew and added, "You won't miss the time I'm gone."

Andrew smiled, too.

Then, Mama came out of her room, dressed to go out.

"Alex, Andrew, I'm leaving. Keep an eye on Bonnie." As she was going downstairs, she said, "I'll be back as soon as I can."

After a while, I heard the storm door hiss shut. I was all alone with Bonnie and Andrew. Bonnie was in her playpen in her room. The house was very quiet. Too quiet.

I was already dressed, ready to go. Andrew leaned against the dresser, still playing with his baseball cap. I felt my hip pocket, making sure my wallet was still there. It was. I eased down on the foot of my bed, so I wouldn't wrinkle the creases in my pants. I looked over at Andrew. He turned the baseball cap in all directions on his head, checked it in the mirror.

"Alex, I've always wanted to be on a real team. I'm finally getting my wish. This is my big chance. You gotta stay with Bonnie."

I jumped up, headed for the door. Andrew ran 'cross the room. He blocked the door.

"And I wanna go get my bike," I said.

I grabbed him, trying to push past. I couldn't. He gripped my shoulders, shoved me back into the room. He started downstairs. I ran after him. I grabbed him by his T-shirt and tugged. I pulled hard until he fell, landed backwards on the floor. There wasn't much room on the landing, but we rolled 'round on it as best as we could. One while, Andrew had me dangling downstairs head first. I tried to flip him, but I only sent him rolling into Bonnie's room.

He landed with a thud against the door. He lay on his back, his feet in the air. The blow made him flip over in such a way that he struck Bonnie's playpen.

Bonnie had started crying. I got off the landing and went in to her.

Andrew saw this as his chance to leave. He picked his cap up, put it on his head, and stumbled downstairs. The old staircase creaked something awful.

I got Bonnie quiet and took her downstairs. But

Andrew was gone. I went outdoors and looked all up and down the street. No Andrew.

In the living room, me and Bonnie must've watched every cartoon in the world. Along about twelve o'clock, I turned the television off and went to fix us some lunch. In the middle of lunch, Mrs. Pettaway came to the door.

Seventeen

Bonnie and I were finishing our tuna sandwiches and milk, when we heard the knock.

"Door," Bonnie said, and took another bite out of her sandwich. The milk had made a moustache on her lip. With a napkin, I wiped it off and went to answer the door.

I thought it'd be Mama coming back early, but it was Mrs. Pettaway. She was dressed the same as always — dark blue dress and white apron. In her hand was a small, thin envelope.

"Alex," she said, when I opened the door. "I got this important-looking letter. For you. The postman put it in with my mail."

I didn't know if it was right or not, but I had to do it. There wasn't any other way. I cleared my throat. "Mrs. Pettaway — "

She didn't answer, but looked at me like she was interested. I took the letter she handed me. It was from the newspaper. Sometimes, they wrote to their newsboys. But it wasn't as important as Mrs. Pettaway thought it was. Just a change in my route.

"I gotta go to town," I said. I held the door for her to come in.

"Cool in here," she said.

"Please sit down," I told her.

When she'd sat down, I said, "I need you to sit with Bonnie."

"Need?" She said it like it was a shock.

I nodded. Maybe she was too old. Too blind.

"Boy, I know what you thinking. I just can't see good enough to read fine print, but I'll be glad to watch Bonnie."

Bonnie'd finished her lunch, so I wiped her mouth and put her in the living room with Mrs. Pettaway. They played patty-cake.

It was 'round two o'clock when I got to the store to get my bike off layaway. It came in a huge cardboard box on account it had to be put together — some parts of it. The clerk told me their man would put it together for another ten dollars. Also, I wouldn't be able to get it until after twelve the following Monday. I'd waited long enough. I had to put it together myself.

Lugging it home from the bus stop was the hardest part. Looking back, I can't remember how

I got it home from the bus stop and 'round to the backyard.

It took the better part of an hour, but I did get it put together without having any extra pieces lying 'round.

I rode my bike down the walk in the backyard just to make sure it was put together right. When I felt like it wasn't gonna fall apart, I rode along the driveway from the garage and headed straight for the vacant lot.

Andrew was still wearing his new baseball cap, and so were the other team members. They were busy playing a game, just getting practice, I guess. Andrew didn't see me. I rode up and down our dead-end street just getting the feel of the new bike.

I pedaled back to the edge of the lot, slowed, and tooted my horn. With all their blue hats gleaming in the afternoon sun, they looked nice, like a real team, like pros. Mac Flemmons was the only one without a baseball cap. He was probably too fat to make the team. He was the first to look up. "Hey! Alex got a new bike!" he yelled.

I tooted my horn again and pedaled back up the street. By the time I turned and was coming back, they were all in the middle of the street.

"Man, that's a neat bike," Sammy said.

"Yeah," Mac agreed, his mouth hanging open like a tired dog.

"I know you gonna let me ride," Mungo said.

"It looks like a racer," Ellis Murdock said. "Is it?"

Before I could answer, Andrew rushed up to me and said, "Let me ride. Let me ride. I'm your brother."

I pedaled 'round to the garage. Andrew dashed after me. "Can I ride?" he asked again.

"Yes, you can ride," I said, laughing, and pedaled back to the street.

"Where you going?" Andrew asked.

I didn't answer, but pedaled slowly up the street.

At the corner, I picked up speed, headed for Thrash Peabody's house, but I could still hear all the great things they were saying about my bike.

Eighteen

"Wow! That's neat!" Thrash said when I got to his house.

"I can't stay long. I'm gonna deliver papers early today."

"Let me try it out," Thrash said, pushing up his glasses.

I got off the bike and Thrash climbed on. Before he pedaled off, I said, "Thrash, why don't you get one of those straps to hold your glasses on?"

"Maybe I will." His house was on a corner. He rode 'round the corner and came back, screeching the tires as he stopped.

"You really got a good one now," he said, smiling.

I got on my bike and started home. Thrash waved. I tooted my horn at him.

When I got back from Thrash's house and was getting ready to go throw papers, Andrew was sitting on the back steps. He was leaning on his hands and looking like his best friend had moved to another city. Since he was so gloomy-looking, it made the red line left over from his swollen eye stand out more, but it'd healed up nicely.

"Hi, Andrew," I said.

He mumbled something and got off the steps to let me into the house.

With my canvas sack fastened to the rack on the fender, I got on my bike and started off. I pedaled over to Andrew. He was sitting on the steps again. "Look, I'll let you ride when I get back."

I didn't wait for him to answer. I pedaled out of the driveway.

Nineteen

It was still pretty early when I got home. I'd almost forgotten about my promise to let Andrew ride my bike. He was over in the lot as usual. I could hear his big mouth even before I pedaled into the driveway.

After I'd parked my bike in the garage and locked it with the new combination lock I'd bought, I went upstairs. I lay on my bed and leafed through comic books I'd already read. Through the open window, I could hear Andrew and the guys shouting at each other.

I'd probably been leafing through the comic books for maybe ten minutes, when I heard a knock at the storm door.

I got up and went to answer it. It was Thrash.

"I took a chance you might be home by now," Thrash said.

When I'd let him in, I said, "What'd you like to do? Go bike riding or over to the lot?"

"Oh, I don't know," Thrash said, pushing up his glasses. "What do you wanna do?"

We were standing in the doorway, trying to decide what to do, when Andrew dashed up on the stoop. He pressed his face against the storm door glass, then opened the door and came in.

"You ready to ride, Andrew?" I asked.

"No. Maybe later." He looked at me, then at Thrash and back to me again. "It's a great-looking bike. But what I need is for you to come get in the game. You, too, Thrash."

I looked at Thrash.

"I will if you will," he said. His glasses slid down, but he didn't push them up.

We went across to the vacant lot. Since I'd delivered the papers so early, so fast, there was plenty of light left for playing ball.

Thrash and I weren't keeping up with Andrew. Not enough to suit Andrew, anyway. When we were almost in the lot, he turned and said, "Hurry up. We need you. Bad."

Twenty

It certainly sounded good to be wanted on a team. But of course Mungo Hubbard was there, and he wasn't too happy when he looked up and saw me and Thrash.

"What is he doing here?" Mungo asked, and jerked his head at me.

Andrew said, "He's gonna play ball. Same as us."

"Naw!" Mungo said. "He can't play. He ain't been playing enough to know how. What you bet, he can't even hit."

Mac and Sammy laughed. In fact, Mac thought it was so funny, he bent over and slapped his thigh. When he'd straightened up, he said, "All them eyes. Bet you can't even see the ball."

Every time he laughed, his stomach rocked like Jell-O.

Then, he said, "Just stick to riding your new bike. Bet you can see how to do that. You don't even need a light for night driving."

"You too fat to run," I told him.

He looked at me. His mouth dropped open. If a feather had fallen from a pigeon flying overhead, it would've sounded like a light bulb crashing on pavement.

Mac still gaped at me. His mouth hung open like a drawbridge in front of a castle. He looked like somebody'd punched him in the stomach.

Mungo went back to center field. "Okay. Let's just play ball. Let Alex and Thrash watch awhile."

"I'm gonna play," I told Andrew.

"Me, too," Thrash said.

Like he was the umpire, Sammy yelled, "Play ball!" To me, he said, "Can you hit? I bet you can't hit."

"If I can't hit the ball, I can hit your big head. It looks like a big brown pumpkin. I bet it'll go squish."

"Here's your chance to find out," Sammy said. "They just retired the side."

Andrew's team whooped and hollered like mad 'cause it was their turn at bat again. There were a lot of bats on the ground in the grass. I picked one up, swung it, just getting the feel of it.

Mungo came up to me, tried to snatch the bat

away, but I held on. His eyes were as big as jumbo-sized eggs when he saw he hadn't taken the bat away from me. He came toward me. "You gonna bat first?"

"Yeah."

Mungo frowned, looked over at Andrew. "We were playing a good game till you came."

Andrew said, "Mungo, what you talking 'bout? We gonna lose this game. Not only does that crosstown team play better than us, but they got us outnumbered."

"Alex can't play ball."

"Let him try. Didn't you try? Besides, we need both of them. Alex and Thrash."

For the longest time, nobody said a word. I was pretty sure they could hear my heart pounding. I looked 'round. Nobody was laughing, so I guess they couldn't.

Mungo edged up close to me and pushed me with his thigh. This time, I glanced over at Andrew. He was just staring like he was watching a movie or something.

"You can take him, Mungo," Mac said.

"Yeah, yeah," Sammy said.

"What we gonna do here? Fight or play ball?" Andrew wanted to know.

I cleared my throat and said to Mungo, "I can fight you or your army. One by one or all together. Either way."

Mungo moved forward a half step. "I don't need

them," he said, waving his bony little arm. He caught me off guard and snatched the bat out of my hand and threw it on the ground. With the toe of his gym shoe, he drew a line in the soft red dirt. "I dare you to cross that line."

I stepped 'cross the line. Mungo drew another. I crossed it. "What're you gonna do, draw or fight?"

Mungo stared at me like he'd never seen me before. He put his hands on my shoulder and pushed. I stepped back. He moved closer. He shoved a bony elbow into my ribs. I got stabbed with an umbrella once. It was a sharp pain. That's what Mungo's elbow felt like.

He stood facing me, quiet. Then, he said, "You could've wrote my essay. You didn't do my sentences, either."

I turned to move away. Mungo grabbed my arm. I pushed him away and grabbed him 'round his chicken neck. I tugged hard and threw him to the ground. We rolled over and over until he was sitting on my chest. It was hard to breathe, and if Mama didn't stick her head out of the door and yell for me soon, she was gonna have only one son.

I looked 'round the crowd, trying to find Andrew. I couldn't. Was he going to let his little brother get beat to a pulp? I couldn't see Thrash, either.

Mungo, still sitting on my chest, asked, "What's the matter?"

"Nothing." I started wriggling, trying to get one

arm loose. I wriggled from side to side, but skinny as he was, he felt like he weighed a ton. What he didn't have in muscle, he made up in height. I wriggled harder. I thought: If I can just shake old Mungo off —

But before I could do anything, Thrash decided to get into the fight. He grabbed Mungo, tried to pull him off me. Mungo poked Thrash with an elbow. Thrash went on pulling at Mungo. He almost pulled Mungo off me, then Mungo jumped up. He picked Thrash up — Thrash was taller than me but not as tall as Mungo — and dumped Thrash into the weeds.

I was halfway up, but before I could stand, Mungo dove at me and pushed me down again.

I was right back where I started. I kept on squirming. Seeing how bad I was struggling, Mungo laughed. I didn't care. I wiggled harder and got my right arm free. I tickled Mungo in the side. He started laughing. I flipped him over, off me. He landed face-first in the soft red dirt.

"You don't fight fair," he sputtered, spitting dirt out of his mouth. He got up, brushed himself off.

"Yes, I do, too. Just as fair as you do." Before I could stand, he grabbed me in a bear hug and threw me back to the ground. We rolled over and over again. I was doomed if I let him get me down again.

With all my strength, I slammed Mungo to the ground. His face and clothes were streaked with red dirt. Mine must've been, too. I held his shoulders flat on the ground and sat on his chest.

"Let me up! Let me up! I don't wanna get all this dirt all over me. I don't want my clothes dirty," Mungo was screaming now. It sounded like he was drowning.

"It's too late. You already dirty." I saw my chance, so I took it. I probably wasn't gonna get another. I bent down, whispered in Mungo's ear. "Tell me your real name." This made him struggle more. I pressed my body down harder on his chest. "It can't be Mungo." I caught his arms, held his wrists. "Tell me."

Since I was sitting on his chest and holding his arms tight, he shook his head from side to side, like his ears were full of sand. He raised his legs and tried to knock me off his chest. I wouldn't budge. "Tell me your name."

I made a fist and was getting ready to sock him on the chin. "Okay. Okay," he said.

In the next moment, Mungo almost twisted free. I did sock him then.

"I'm bleeding. My mouth is bleeding."

"Your name, Mungo."

He shook his head from side to side. "Don't tell anybody." I saw pleading, fear in his eyes. I leaned forward, my ear close to Mungo's mouth. "Solomon Bartholomew Hubbard."

Slowly, I got off his chest and let him up. I started laughing. I ran 'round the field hopping on one foot. And laughing. That's when I saw

Thrash still poking 'round in the weeds.

Just as I was about to go over to Thrash, see if he was all right, he held up his glasses. They'd come off when Mungo threw him into the weeds. His glasses had fallen apart.

"Alex, I'm going home. Gotta screw my glasses back together." I watched Thrash as he went on 'cross the street.

Over in the south end of the lot where the grass grew taller — maybe four feet or more, I saw Solomon Bartholomew Hubbard breaking off wide blades of grass and dabbing at his clothes. He'd worn a white T-shirt and beige jeans. They were streaked with red dirt. It was caked on his clothes. Rubbing his clothes with the grass like that was only making matters worse. Now they were getting all streaked with green grass stains.

"You better be glad I don't want to get dirty," he said, scowling at me.

I didn't say anything. Later, Andrew would say I stood there looking at Mungo with a silly grin on my face. I looked 'round, trying to find Andrew. It seemed like lately all I'd been doing was try to find Andrew.

He came over to me. He put his hand on my shoulder. Grinning, he said, "Let's go home."

I walked slowly out of the lot, while Andrew bounced along beside me. "Race you," I said, smiling.

I looked back in time to see Mungo trotting

119

'cross the other end of the lot, headed home. "Andrew? Loser wash and dry the dishes for a week."

He was grinning, sure of himself. "No. Let's go for the big stakes. Loser wash and dry the dishes for a whole month."

We shook hands. "You're on."

Crashing through weeds as he went, Andrew tore off for the edge of the vacant lot. His legs were longer than mine and he had a head start, but I was ready. I took a deep breath and started running. If I stretched my legs any more, they'd have been made of rubber.

I could feel the sun burning on my neck. Sweat poured down my back and face. With the back of my hand, I wiped my face and didn't stop running.

I caught Andrew and passed him as he reached the sidewalk in front of our house.

I tore open the storm door, ran inside. I latched the door so Andrew couldn't get in. "I won! I won!" I shouted.

He tugged at the door, found it latched. He was too winded to do anything. He sat on the top step until he got his wind back. He wiped a bucket of sweat off his forehead onto the front of his T-shirt.

"All right," he gasped. "You the best."

I unlatched the door, went out. We shook hands again, then I went upstairs, bathed, and changed.

Twenty minutes later, I was laying on my bed reading a space comic book I'd already read a hundred times. Andrew slumped down in the big chair Mama'd given us when she got new furniture for the living room.

Andrew swung his left leg over the arm of the chair. He was swinging his leg a mile a minute.

"You know, you a real hero, Alex. I guess maybe I was a teeny bit jealous. I don't know what I would've done about Mrs. Pettaway. You a real hero." Andrew laughed and swung his foot.

We were quiet then, the only sound was of him swinging his foot, a kind of swishing sound.

"Anything you saw you wanted, you went after it till you got it. Stuck to things till they were finished. I can't remember the number of times I've tried delivering papers and stopped. I'll never forget the fire. Not ever." Andrew laughed. He sat up, swung his right leg over the chair some.

I waited for him to say something else. I didn't have any idea what to say. Andrew still liked me, I was thinking. I shook my head, clearing it.

He kept on grinning and swinging his foot. "Look at the way you went on reading to Mrs. Pettaway even when the guys teased you like crazy. I even teased you, but you didn't stop. I would've stopped. Reading to her, I mean."

"I don't think you would've." I said. Andrew didn't say anything. He simply went on grinning, swinging his foot.

We sat in our room and remembered things and didn't even think about beating each other up; then, Mama called us down to supper.

About the Author

Johnniece Marshall Wilson has stacked veneer, typed in a wholesale jeweler's, sold encyclopedias, and delivered newspapers. Now she is a food service worker at John Kane Hospital in Pittsburgh, Pennsylvania.

She says "I was writing a story about a boy who runs away from home, but I abandoned it because there was a real big game in the middle of the street and I wanted to see it. I never did go outdoors because I had another idea about what I really wanted to write. So I wrote a story about two brothers who didn't play ball together — they were too busy fighting."

Johnniece Marshall Wilson lives with her three daughters in Wilkinsburg, Pennsylvania. This is her first novel.